LORD WINTERTON'S SECRET

Virtue Browne was once childhood friends with the mysterious Lord Winterton. But now villagers avoid the crumbling wreck of his manor house on the dunes, and gossips whisper that the young lord is involved in arcane rituals. A headstrong governess, too inquisitive for her own good, Virtue will encounter romance, mystery and smugglers at her first posting. Is there a logical explanation for the strange things she sees? Or will she become another soul lost in the rumoured secret tunnels?

KITTY-LYDIA DYE

♦

LORD WINTERTON'S SECRET

LINFORD
Leicester

First published in Great Britain in 2022

First Linford Edition
published 2022

A catalogue record for this book is available
from the British Library.

ISBN 978–1–4448–4955–4

Published by
Ulverscroft Limited
Anstey, Leicestershire

Printed and bound in Great Britain by
TJ Books Ltd., Padstow, Cornwall

This book is printed on acid-free paper

A Phantom

Villagers never strayed near Lord Winterton's manor on these Norfolk dunes. They treated him like a folk legend, a warning to stay indoors at night.

Old Ben, the lighthouse-keeper, slurped his blackberry syrup and kept watch, not only for ships weaving in the ribbon-like waves but also for any stray lambs. It was a heavy duty.

Ben's lips puckered with distaste as the young lord appeared, draped in a cape harshly buffeted by winds. He was as handsome as he was wicked, tall and slim with a sorrowful sort of face.

He strode against the elements, the rattle of his lantern resembling a chuckling skull, and vanished inside the dark maw of the tunnels beneath the sands.

Then came howls and shrieks, inhuman and desperate.

Ben shuddered. None could halt this phantom in his pleasures. They only

1

hoped he would grow bored and depart to hunt for more enticing victims.

★　★　★

'There's nothing shameful about being a governess, Father!' 'There is when you're spreading harmful ideology to impressionable girls.'

'Mary Anning's fossil hunting is hardly —' Virtue Browne looked heavenward and changed tack. 'There is more harm in being kept ignorant. A woman needs to know more than dancing, diction and delicacy.'

Her father scoffed and resumed staring out of the coach window.

Virtue sighed. She was exhausted; they'd not stopped since leaving Yarmouth.

The coast was beautiful even under this dull sky. Cottages were sparse smatterings of flint and thatch.

The sight of her childhood home offered some comfort. During their missionary work there had been misery and distrust from people who wanted to be left alone.

Virtue and her father were no longer welcome in 1820s China.

She saw, up on the dunes, the manor house, her new home. Set apart from the rest of the village it clung like kelp suckered to stone. One fearsome storm might tip it into the sea taking everyone with it.

Virtue chafed her cold arms. This would be her first posting yet that was not why her heart pounded.

August Winterton was no stranger. With so few children in the village they had often played together with Jeb Straw-house, the son of a local fisherman. They would be out from sunrise to sunset, the two older boys' shadows merging with hers upon the sands.

August was a quiet boy. It was Virtue who pulled him into their games, while he would rather investigate the rock-pools.

It wasn't that he ignored her. He treated her as gently as the seashells they collected, his pale cheeks reddening whenever she kissed one in thanks.

Jeb, on the other hand, knew nothing of softness. He'd shout and laugh over August like a gull drowning out whispering waves.

Virtue did not know if August would remember her. She shifted, uncertain how to act when they came face to face.

Children were blind to the rigid structures of society. Now she was a woman she could not ignore what made them different. She was a governess and he a lord.

'We made good time,' Virtue commented. 'I can get acquainted with Miss Winterton before we start our work.'

'A day early?' Her father spotted something emerging ahead. 'Do you want to be considered too keen? They won't expect you yet. You'll be an inconvenience.'

Virtue's mouth settled into a thin line.

'I think the master would be pleased. From what the steward wrote there has been no female influence for several years.'

'Staff shouldn't be gossiping. A man and his servant should be the same as a confessor and his priest.'

He made a faint wheezing sound.

'I need to stretch my legs; get some fresh air. You'll not force an old man further than he's able?'

Yet he hefted his walking stick with ease to strike the roof. The coach jolted to a stop. Her father threw open the door and hobbled out.

Virtue gritted her teeth as she, too, disembarked. She had spotted the inn on the seafront with its seagull-painted sign.

'One drink!' she called to her father's retreating back.

When had her feelings towards him become so disillusioned? Perhaps every woman relinquished her heartstrings to make room for a future husband.

The distance between them would therefore be her fault rather than Father's callousness.

Colour fled her cheeks, kissed away by

the chill of the winds. Virtue gazed past the inn, focusing on a strip of sea fringed by marram grasses.

She would walk along the beach. Far better to breathe in salt winds rather than the beer-tinged smoke of the inn.

There might even be a path to the manor. She doubted she would make a good impression, however, if she were to arrive ruddy-faced and panting, heaving her luggage with sand encrusting her hair and seaweed caught on her shoe.

The image brought back her smile.

Lord Winterton would turn her out before she had even begun her work!

An Old Friend

Sea foam pooled amongst stones, bubbles bursting to leave a shimmer of wetness.

The warm winds stirred the sand, spraying it back and forth as if the ground moved with Virtue.

As a girl she would kick off her boots and race, hair streaming and skirts tangling. Her toes twitched; the urge was still there.

Footsteps crunched behind her and she turned, shielding her eyes with her glove. A broad silhouette strode over with something ragged as seaweed swinging from his shoulder.

'It can't be little Virtue?' the stranger said in the Norfolk accent she herself had lost.

His face was tanned by the sun, pale hair wild. Strong, weathered hands clutched his nets, which bulged with dredged mussels.

Familiarity tugged at her yet the

memory was unable to resurface. She gave the stranger an awkward smile.

He rubbed a scar on his chin.

'I can't blame a girl for forgetting when she's had the whole world to explore. Though maybe it's more to do with you wanting to forget what you did to me.'

Her eyes focused upon the red, jagged strip of flesh. Heat squirmed its way to her throat and cheeks.

'It can't be! I didn't leave such a mark.'

But with time the scar would have stretched, growing with its owner.

She stared at the freckled face and the man looked back with crinkled blue eyes.

There was only one other boy whose eyes she had ever bothered to gaze into.

'Jeb!' She made to embrace him, but the warning twinge of her stays stopped her.

She was a woman now. Respectable women did not throw themselves at men, whatever their pasts.

The last time they had seen one another they had retreated from the fierce sun into the cool shadows of a cave. Water was gently sloshing as they made their way to the small stone island in its centre.

While she was distracted by glimmers of light reflected upon the walls Jeb had leaned over and pressed his mouth to hers.

Virtue had shoved him, then cried out in horror as he toppled, fell against the rocks and stayed there.

She went running for help, not waiting to see him get up, bloodied and laughing — another of his mischiefs.

Now Jeb was before her, a man, yet he still had the smile that made her want to laugh.

'It's a wonder you can smile at me,' she told him.

'It was my fault, I suppose, surprising you like that. What has brought you back?'

'My father tired of teaching overseas. I am to be a governess.'

A pucker formed between his eyebrows.

'So Winterton's lured you home. There

will just be him, a few servants and the little girl to keep you company.'

Jeb seemed unwilling to speak any more about the matter. He hefted his nets and started walking. Virtue followed.

'How have you fared?' she asked. 'Are you now a fisherman, like your father?'

'I've risen up, as you have. I went on the trawlers with him and learned all his tricks. The old cutthroat drowned when I was eighteen.'

'I'm sorry.'

She struggled to keep pace, her much smaller feet stepping in the large imprints of his footsteps in the sand.

'He was so drunk he fell overboard before we set sail. I left the sea once I had enough saved and bought the inn from Zachariah.'

They were heading for the Seagull's Retreat where her father had hastened to.

'You own it now?'

He grunted in affirmation as they made their way up the path between the dunes.

'I've taken in some of our injured boys from Waterloo. Seeing as they don't have everything they need to work on the boats, at least this gives them something to do rather than stewing.'

Many had been severely wounded in the battle of Waterloo nine years ago. When those brave men returned home they often found the rest of the world had moved on.

Seagulls shrieked overhead. Waves crashed, distant yet also overbearingly loud.

'Where's your father?' Jeb said.

'In your inn,' she admitted reluctantly.

'You did not fancy it? I'm sure I have something collecting dust that'll suit a gentler pair of lips.'

Her cheeks were turning red again though she pretended they were not.

'Thank you, but I'm afraid we must continue our journey. The manor is still a good distance away.'

'It'll be dark by the time you arrive. You shouldn't be there, not on your first —'

11

Jeb looked to the skies; the clouds were as thick as cloth.

'Storm's coming. I feel it in my bones. Lord Winterton can wait another night for you.'

His smile was gone, his eyes shadowy. Virtue realised he was almost imploring her to stay.

Dread lurched at what he hinted at. In the distance, the manor seemed like a hulking beast lying in wait for prey.

She scrabbled for an excuse.

'It would not be proper for me to be here, even with my father.'

'We're an inn. Plenty women bed here for the night.'

Jeb was all cheer again.

'I tell you, a duchess once roomed here in disguise to track down her runaway husband.

'I also employ an old widow. Will she be chaperone enough for you?'

As children she, August and Jeb had had no chaperones.

Virtue watched the skies in her turn.

There was her duty to consider. Her

future.

'Thank you, Jeb,' she said finally as they passed the inn's threshold. 'It would, no doubt, be better if I arrived after a good night's rest.

'I know nothing of what has happened in the village since I left. Perhaps you can tell me?'

A Harsh Judge

The inn was made of flint and ships' timbers with few windows. Carvings of fish and sea monsters were affixed to the walls and draped in old nets.

Smoke tickled Virtue's throat and the heady, almost sticky vapour of beer dampened her cheek.

A shaggy-haired dog lay before a fire which crackled and popped. Its eye cracked open to appraise her.

'Get back to sleep, Shuck,' Jeb said, nudging the dog's side with his boot. The dog snorted and curled in on himself.

Virtue's father sat at the bar. Several empty tankards surrounded him.

She scowled, but he had yet to notice.

He was attended to by a young man missing his left arm. The boy met Jeb's eye and grinned.

'There, now,' he joked, 'it's the Lord of the Sea come back with his spoils.'

Finally, her father noticed them. His eyes narrowed in confusion.

Jeb cheerily cocked his head.

'How are you, old man? Have another drink on me.'

Virtue's father drained his cup and Jeb bent down to her.

'All this time and now I've discovered his weakness.'

He went into the back room to put away his nets, nodding a greeting to the barman.

When he returned, rolling out the ache in his shoulders, he carried a glass decanter filled with a wheat-yellow liquid.

'Sherry. The duchess I told you about left me this as a thank you. Give it a try.'

They sat at one of the tables. A snake's carving with a knotted tail sneered above Jeb.

Virtue tried a sip of the sherry. It was sweet yet slightly sharp. Her mouth pursed.

'You've turned out mighty fine, Virtue, even if you are kitted out so severely. You'd do better to wear blue.'

'You've become . . .' She wanted to

return the compliment, yet was uncertain how without it sounding forward. 'You're not a boy any more.'

'Indeed I am not!' He chuckled.

They talked about what Virtue had seen during her travels and the more interesting guests Jeb had hosted.

Each time she attempted to glean whether August and Jeb remained friends he nudged the conversation elsewhere.

It was beginning to frustrate her.

Outside, the sky turned the colour of wet stone, throbbing and pulsing. A rumble dragged over the waves. The inn sign rattled, chain twisting.

When the first boom sounded Shuck raised his head, groaning low in mimicry. Fishermen came in to wait out the storm.

Quite a bit of sherry had been drunk. Virtue had no idea how it had happened yet her laughter came more easily.

'You've been dodging and ducking all night.' Her voice sounded strange in her ears. 'Tell me something about August.

'This secretive nonsense is making me

think he's a wolf in man's flesh!'

'Perhaps he is.' This was no joke. Jeb's tone had darkened. 'I shudder at the thought of you alone with him.'

'There will be servants!'

'In his employ. Even if they were honest folk, I doubt he would pay them much mind. Life is replaceable to him.

'Did you know he's the local magistrate for the Assizes?'

'Well, but surely he cannot go against the law?'

'Oh, no, he sticks to the letter, but he relishes his work. If he can give a harsh sentence, he will.

'Lashings. Pillory. A friend of mine was hanged.'

Her hand shot out, curling around Jeb's wrist. Its warmth scalded her palm, hairs tickling between her fingers.

'There were tigers where I lived in China and they did not frighten me. Besides, if I called for you, you'd come rescue me.'

'That I would, princess. Be sure to call loud enough so I hear you on the winds.'

He knocked back the rest of his drink. 'Winterton always gives me a bitter taste.'

Their conversation had soured as well. A cold dread lapped at Virtue's innards as she anticipated tomorrow's meeting with her old friend.

'I think I'd best head to bed.'

Virtue made to rise but stumbled. Jeb's hands circled her waist, breath fluttering on the nape of her neck.

Somehow, she managed to get upstairs. There were no other guests so she had been given the room with the best view, not that she was in her right senses to enjoy this.

She sank upon the bed, thinking it the comfiest thing in the world.

As her head nestled into the pillow she realised she had forgotten to say goodnight to Jeb.

A Winning Kiss

Virtue woke with a jolt, sweat gleaming on her cheek. Quickly her nightmare slithered from her though those fragments she recalled made her throat lurch — a wolf bursting out of a man while a figure with Jeb's grinning face swung from a gibbet.

'I'll never drink sherry again,' she vowed.

She watched the storm through the window. Sand-whipped dunes rustled as if an army marched on them. The full moon hung clear while the dark around it writhed.

Her tongue was dry and, more than anything, she needed the privy. Below her she heard the rough murmur of voices.

Stealthily, she went downstairs. Jeb was still up. He held a shot of whisky and a fan of cards clamped in his other hand. Concentration furrowed his face.

Three other men sat with him.

Fishermen, most likely. They must be the same age yet the whittling of the sea winds had made them haggard.

In hushed tones they argued. Virtue thought she heard mention of crops being sowed. She leaned against the banister to hear better, then the wood traitorously groaned.

Jeb's head whipped up.

'Miss Browne, you should be asleep!'

The door slammed open as another customer entered. Rainwater slid from the stranger's cape and his boots squelched as he made his way to the bar.

Virtue was too embarrassed to ask Jeb where the privy was situated.

'The storm woke me.' she said, hating how like a frightened child she sounded.

'It'll have slunk off by daybreak, best sleep it through.' Jeb crooked his finger. 'But before you do, I'm on a losing streak. Won't you blow a kiss upon my cards? I'll be the luckiest man in the room.'

She could have snapped at him for putting her on the spot and flounced back to bed, yet the curious, slightly hostile but appreciative stares of the men made her come down, approaching unsteadily.

The cards were held out and Virtue bent her head, a loose lock of hair tumbling. Her lips puckered and blew.

Jeb's arm snaked around her waist.

'Shall we see how good your luck is?'

The game they were playing was whist. Jeb showed his hand. He and his partner had the most tricks. Piles of coins and bags of tobacco were at his side.

Another round was dealt. This time he lost and, as easily as drawing breath, the coins were taken.

'You've near cleared me out, lads,' Jeb said cheerfully. 'But I've one more thing of value to put upon the table — dear Virtue.'

Shocked, she pictured herself being thrust upon the sticky table, scattering the cards and coins and gin.

'Whoever wins gets a kiss,' Jeb offered.

She glanced around for her father and spotted him. She made to call for his help, then noticed how he was slumped. Slowly he slid to the floor.

It had been the same in China, his promises to her as insubstantial as sea froth.

This had to be a jest! Any moment Jeb would give her a smile and let her go.

The stranger had joined the table. A gloved hand picked up the cards, fingers crooked and unsteady as if in pain.

Jeb's arm, still around her, went taut.

The stranger did not look at what he had been dealt, merely set the cards upon the table face down.

'Well?' he enquired, voice smooth. 'You have offered quite a prize, though I think it one that was not yours to gamble.'

'Are you all bark? Will you fold?'

Jeb snarled and revealed his hand.

'I win!'

'I'm afraid not.'

Rescuer or Reprobate?

The stranger said no more, merely rose. He looked at Virtue and she knew he had seen her flinch. He held out his arm, indicating to the inn door for her to follow.

'I think it best we step outside. It is too close and loud for what I have in mind.'

There was nowhere to run! Her useless, selfish father, still snored on the floor.

Only she could save herself.

As Virtue made for the door Jeb clumsily reached for her.

'Virtue, I only meant — it was a joke!'

Her palm struck his cheek, the force of it turning his head aside.

'It only became a joke when you lost!' she hissed.

As all gazes were still on Jeb's florid cheek no-one noticed her snatch a knife from the table and hide it in her skirts.

Outside, the night shimmered with needle shards of pounding rain. The stranger held his cape over Virtue's head, protecting her from the worst of the elements.

A horse tethered there was shifting, desperate to be off again. It was as black as the night, a giant with rippling muscles and tendrils of ink for a mane.

The glistening hooves stamped; the head tossed, nostrils flaring.

Virtue gripped her knife tighter.

'I'm not some prize — some object — to be passed back and forth,' she said.

She would not tremble.

'Do you think me about to carry you away to the fairy hills?'

She could not tell if he spoke in anger or jest. He bent his head and she tilted hers to look at him.

He gave her a soft smile.

'There is no need to fear me,' he told her. 'I have never meant you harm.'

He took her hand tenderly and she knew she could trust him. The knife fell on the sands.

He placed a frigid kiss upon her knuckles. When he released her she was clutching something else: a ring.

It was a silver band with an orange and red-speckled jewel. Tiny detailing resembled grasping thorns.

He settled his cape around her shoulders.

'You should not remain here. Will you not come with me? I only offer shelter.'

She was tempted but must deal with Jeb.

'My father is within. I will leave in the morning.'

'Then I hope to see you again soon.'

He strode over to the horse, calming it with a single stroke to its nose.

'Come, Ragnar.'

He jerked the rope free and swung himself up, riding without a saddle. Though storms lashed the dunes and the sea clapped its hands in fury he rode into the dying night, merging with the other shadows.

Virtue pulled the cape around herself. The rain ran through her hair and lapped at her cheeks.

She almost believed he had not truly

been there. However, the ring was proof.

Laughter snapped from within the inn. Clearly they had already forgotten what had transpired.

Virtue turned as crooked, wrinkled hands gripped her.

An old woman stood, neck twisted to stare up at her. Her silvery eyes peered from folds of flesh and layers of ragged shawls.

'Do not go near him!' she cried.

'What?' Virtue asked, astounded.

'My man is in there, befuddled and slurring, though he never touches a drop when it's his turn to man the lighthouse.

'He has seen evil upon the dunes, in the tunnels in the sands, yet no-one does anything. They are too frightened!'

'Come in to the warmth,' Virtue urged. 'That creature you allowed to touch you worships sea spirits! He charms women and lures them to his rituals at the full moon.

'We hear screams, then screeching, scraping noises within the dunes as though these women are clawing to get out!'

26

'Please, calm yourself. This man . . .'

But dread unravelled inside of Virtue. She had known all along.

'He is Lord Winterton, the beast of this coast!' the old woman cried.

* * *

Virtue went to her room and barricaded herself in. Sleep would not come.

August had been her rescuer, easily resettling into the role after so many years! He remembered her.

He had also witnessed the shameful way Jeb had treated her. He must think her a woman of loose morals.

Yet what the locals said of him was no better. 'The beast, Lord Winterton'.

It had been a mistake to return here. Nothing was how she imagined it would be.

She would not run, she decided finally. She would not throw aside this opportunity because of idle gossip.

She rose before daybreak. The storm had abated. She peered in her father's room to find him on the floor snoring.

Outside, the coach driver was setting up. He heaved himself into his seat and Virtue opened the door to climb inside.

'We will be setting off now,'she called, grim-mouthed.

'Do we not wait for the old man, miss?'

'He will be remaining here.'

On the journey she went through her arrival a dozen times in her mind, from the mundane worry of tripping over her skirt to the more anxious fear of an instant dismissal.

There was the even wilder possibility of Lord Winterton grasping her hand and dragging her to those rumoured tunnels.

Virtue scolded herself. If there was risk of tripping she could raise her skirts, as long as no-one caught the flash of her ankle.

Should Lord Winterton dismiss her she would explain the chain of events leading to what transpired.

To the final doubt, the one she pushed aside as foolish but which was the most vividly painted, she had no answer.

Jeb had not cared about her feelings. Why should August be any different?

Virtue straightened up, positive that, whatever came at her, she would find a way of turning it to her advantage.

Her years in China had prepared her. A man was no different than a tiger, though not as beautiful or graceful as those majestic creatures.

So focused was she on her plan of attack that she barely noticed the emerging sunlight striking the stretch of beach they drove past.

The sea was calm and steady like a length of shimmering blue material rolled out. Red-beaked terns burst from the dune grasses to gently bob upon the water.

Instead, what she gazed upon was Winterton Manor. Steadying her bonnet, she leaned out of the window to watch.

She wondered which member of the Winterton family had been headstrong enough to think he could live here.

The sand cliff it had been built on had

eroded, the land beneath either crumbling or already scattered on the beach below.

There was a sadness about the place, if a building could have feelings. The west wing reminded her of a husk of a chrysalis, the butterfly long departed. It was such an awful shame to let this go to ruin.

Then the coach pulled up and she could no longer put this off.

She did not even make it to the steps, guarded by hunched stone mythical creatures she recognised as wyverns, before a small figure in white darted to meet her, a servant following.

Imogen Winterton's honey-hued hair haloed her cherubic cheeks and wide blue eyes as she floated across to her.

Virtue had hoped for a smiling face. Instead, the child's expression was as frigid as a doll's.

'Welcome to Winterton Manor,' the child intoned, her tiny lace gloves clasped together, chin upturned. 'A room has been set aside for you.'

A single flick of her fingers and the man rushed over to carry Virtue's bags.

'It's a pleasure to meet you.' Virtue dipped slightly. 'Is your father at home? I would like to see him.'

Some emotion showed then. A furrow of annoyance appeared between Imogen's eyebrows and her cheeks puffed.

'Papa is very busy. When he is ready to see you I will let you know.'

The message was clear. Before the child could order her inside Virtue knew she must show where each stood in this hierarchy.

'Very well, then we'll go to the classroom. I wish to get started straightaway.'

She held out her hand and grinned down at her.

Imogen hesitated and, ever so slightly, her lip wobbled.

Her hand darted out, clinging to what Virtue offered.

No Longer Children

Something disturbed August in his work — the arrival of the coach. He lifted the curtain to get a better look.

Imogen had been furious to learn he had spoken with the new governess before her. She had forbidden him from seeing her again, at least until tonight.

Luckily, August hadn't mentioned their previous association as heaven knew how Imogen would react.

His idle comment last night, sitting by the fire to chase off the chill while she fussed over him, had angered the girl. He struggled to recall what he'd even said.

Now he saw Miss Browne alight from the coach. Last night's reunion with her had been in the shadowy caresses of candlelight, but the blazing sunlight did not diminish her radiance.

'I never dared hope you would return,' he murmured.

He had predicted the flushed-faced girl, full of vibrancy, would grow into a beautiful woman. It often came to him in passing, fondly remembering the past before bitterness drowned his youthful innocence.

The fracture had begun when Virtue left.

August had run to the beach as usual, needing to see her, clutching the special treasure he had found.

Jeb was there, violently skipping stones. A fresh scar gleamed on his chin.

'She's gone,' he had spat. 'You'll not see her again!'

Somehow he had known the other boy must be at fault. They had rolled about, trading blows, until Jeb ran off.

August had staggered home, shirt torn and one eye squinting shut. His father had been waiting, lip curled with disdain.

'Are both my children to be disappointments?'

A place was soon found at boarding-school. Not once did August consider returning, instead signing up with the Army when he was old enough.

Finally his responsibilities became

impossible to ignore, pulling him back here. Whatever took place in this house would be down to him.

When he realised who had answered his advertisement he could have rejected Virtue but he had not and was unable to say why.

The tightening in his chest as he watched from the window gave no clues.

He was too far away to catch her expression as she took in the house. Her head tilted, no doubt with that determination he had admired last night.

His fingers, for once bare but kept in the shadows of the room, curled. A spasm stiffened the muscles in his wrist. It felt as if thorns dragged beneath his flesh.

August gritted his teeth against the pain even as the nerves in his hands tremored, beginning to lock. He was helpless against his own body.

He made to set the book upon his desk as his vision grew hazy. It fell, scattering loose pages covered in rough scratches.

He shut his eyes and smothered his

frustration as he seated himself with his back to the loveliness he had been studying.

He was no longer the man he had been. Only a shade remained, burdened by regrets and surrounded by enemies.

August might avoid her for now but he would have to see Virtue at some point.

He owed her an explanation. No doubt she had been besieged by rumours about him already, possibly even the truth.

She was brave to have come here, just as she had been as a girl. Always the first to run into the dark recesses of caves.

He must leave her alone. They were not children any more. She was here to be housed, employed and protected, nothing else.

Tigers and Tea

Imogen led Virtue to where their classes would be held. Their footsteps echoed through dark corridors, lit only by stray shards of light coming through the curtains.

This was the first time Virtue had been inside the manor. As a girl she'd begged August to sneak her in with him but it was the only place he would not share.

Silence was demanded here — a sickly relative who could not be disturbed. Virtue wondered if the person still lived.

Portraits of women long dead peered at her from over fans or bare shoulders. One painting, of a satyr disturbing a group of dancing nymphs, made her eyes widen.

'Is your father an art collector?'

'He collects beautiful things,' the child said. 'We have the garden and its statues.' 'You must show me another day. Do you and your father walk around there often?'

'My father is not your concern. You are here to teach me, are you not?'

Virtue almost reprimanded the child for her rudeness, then considered the reason for this hostility. Having never had to share her father, might Imogen think her a threat to his affections?

'That is true, Imogen, but your father will want to know how you are doing.'

'You will tell him if I'm badly behaved?'

'I am hopeful I will only be telling him about the times you are good.'

They entered the study. The windows had been thrown open to let in a sea breeze.

Below was a stretch of sea close enough one could almost climb out and dive in.

Books lined the shelves. There were novels with names such as '*The Abbey Of Gloaming*' and '*Ghosts Of The Locked Chamber*' as well as tomes of the Grecian gods and Viking sagas.

Virtue gasped. Books were special to her. Not many could be carried when she and her father had been travelling.

To see so many books in one place and

within reach filled her with joy.

Upon the desk lay a rather detailed model of a woman reclining. Virtue removed her pelisse and covered the work of art.

'From my understanding,' she began, 'you are knowledgeable in Norse legends?'

'My father reads me stories from his books. Did you know the goddess Freyja had a chariot pulled by cats? And Viking women went to battle as shield maidens?'

'You cannot be loyal to just one subject, Miss Winterton. What of the Egyptians? The Romans?'

Imogen shook her head.

'When I was in China the people believed amber carried a tiger's soul along with its strength and bravery,' Virtue told her.

'You have travelled, miss?'

Gone was Imogen's haughtiness. The mask fell to reveal an inquisitive child.

Virtue told her of blistering heat followed by monsoons, the people and cultures she met and her encounter with a tiger.

'Were you not scared?'

'I was more afraid of our guide. He was a man intent on adventure and I feared he would provoke the beast into lunging.

'The tiger was majestic; graceful and yet deadly. As I urged Mr Rafe to be still and quiet it slipped back into the under-growth as quietly as a snake.'

They discussed the anatomy of tigers and what happened to bones over years, which led to Virtue introducing the sub-ject of Mary Anning's fossils at Lyme Regis.

The sky had turned the colour of amber.

'This was . . .' the girl paused. 'I do not have the word. I cannot remember —'

'It was lovely meeting you, too, Imo-gen. I hope it will be the same tomorrow.'

The girl dipped in a curtsey and hur-ried to go and play. Virtue put away the books, papers and inkwell.

Today had gone quite well. Now she

must wait to see whether Lord Winterton would demand her presence.

Virtue longed to explore the manor but did not know where she was allowed. The house's creaks, cracks and shifting also made her fear she might end up somewhere unstable.

She watched from the window as the sun disappeared into the sea. A clock chimed.

There came a tap on the door. Imogen, bleary-eyed, stood in slippers and nightdress.

'Papa has asked for you.' Her hand lifted to stifle her yawn. 'He is in the library.'

Virtue led the girl to her room and bade her goodnight, then went in search of the library. She pulled her shawl closer.

What frustrated her most was that she still did not have a clear picture of who August was now. What had happened to the sweet boy she once knew?

After everything she had heard she wanted to form her own opinion.

A fire had been lit in the library. The

gold titles of the books glimmered. Within a cabinet were silhouettes of leering wooden figures and masks.

She stepped into the room and Lord Winterton arose from the sofa. Much too close. She started backing away until she was caged against the bookshelf.

Virtue tilted her head defiantly as she noticed bright amusement in his eyes.

'Please sit, Miss Browne. A drink?'

'No.' She was remembering the sherry.

'It is only tea.'

On the small table stood tea pot and cups. No servant was in attendance and she was surprised to see him serve.

When she tried to help he waved her off but his grip was rigid and he wore gloves. A muscle twitched in his cheek, caused by a furled knot in his jaw.

'I must warn you,' August said, 'I am not one for social convention. In London I am avoided due to my eccentricities.'

His lip twisted sardonically.

'August —' She halted. It was better to remain formal. 'Lord Winterton, I have heard rumours about you.'

'And these rumours are?' His eyes narrowed but his voice remained silky.

'An old woman in the village called you a monster, sir. Apparently you lure and torture women for rituals!'

He could not help laughing. At how seriously she repeated this, at how pale her cheek was even though she pretended not to believe such things.

He stopped as he saw her cringe.

'Then what I said to you last night no doubt added fuel to the fire! I am not a druid, if that is what you fear. They think me strange because I prefer to remain here with my solitude and statues.

'When Imogen's mother perished my priorities settled into place.'

Virtue shook herself. She had been foolish to consider the rumours true. They might have come from the pages of a novel.

He was only a widower wanting to do best by his daughter.

'Thank you for helping me last night. I am sorry you had to involve yourself. Jeb was in his cups and it was a joke gone too far.'

'I'd be more careful with who you keep as friends. Jebediah Strawhouse is no longer the boy we knew. You'd best avoid him.'

'Why?'

He did not answer and she pressed him. 'Jeb said much the same about you but would not divulge his reasons. Though, yes, I do not plan on speaking with him again.'

She was not sure Jeb could ever regain her trust. She changed the subject.

'Imogen is a fast learner and inquisitive. I will enjoy teaching her. May I ask what made you introduce her to Viking tales?'

'It is a subject which fascinates me. Did you know the land here was once taken control of by marauding Vikings, who soon formed a settlement?

'My family has lived here for generations.

Perhaps it is the warrior in my blood wanting to relive the glory days. Mary

Anning's discoveries are just as intriguing.'

'You were listening to us?'

'I work in the room above yours. As both of our windows were open I could not help but enjoy your lesson as well.'

She swallowed hard. Wherever she went it seemed August would know.

'May I ask what it is you do?'

They had been as close as this last night, but in whipping wind. Now, in the caressing warmth of a fire, his scent crept up.

It was a pleasant one. There was something of the woods about him, a forest in winter, cool nights of frost and bitter berries, overwhelmed by a smoky smell.

She thought it might come from the firewood in the grate. It was seductive.

'I'm not wasting my inheritance as the rakes in London do. I invest, mainly in hospitals.' His hands rubbed together. 'I'm afraid it is very boring. Tales of legendary heroes vanquishing monsters at least spice the tedium of life.'

'I am surprised you wish your daughter

to learn of such things. Most would rather focus on good manners.'

'Lest her poor, fragile girl's mind will crumble? I do not believe this foolish notion that a woman is unable to comprehend basic things. I will deny Imogen nothing.

'As I have no sons I need her capable of succeeding me, whatever society says.'

'That is . . .'

Virtue's father's voice was coming back to her. Each time he'd confiscated her books for fear Mary Wollstonecraft's words might corrupt her development.

When she had told him she wished to study as a governess he had railed at her.

Why could she not serve as his housekeeper, or marry a teacher and assist him? What could she hope to achieve while she left hearth and kitchen unattended?

As she hesitated gloved fingers ghosted over her face. She stiffened, tea spilling into her saucer as his thumb traced the curve of her cheek.

It sent a thrill through her. But his eyes

seemed glazed as though in a trance.

Could no man be trusted? A common mongrel had more restraint!

She would not stand for this. She leaped up, setting down her teacup hard. 'Good night, sir.'

She hurried for the door.

Lord Winterton remained seated, his hand still raised.

After Waterloo

Curses! What had he done this time? The poppy tincture August had taken still left a bitter flavour upon his tongue.

He forced down his now cold tea, trying to clear the fugue ensnaring his mind.

He had been conversing politely with Miss Browne, he was sure, although perhaps divulging more than he had wanted to.

It was difficult not to, when she looked at him with such curiosity.

Then he had . . .

His hand clenched into a fist and he gritted his teeth against the pain.

'Fool!' he hissed.

It had been the way the firelight illuminated her face. August had thought he had been admiring the vision before him in his mind. Yet his traitorous body . . .

Virtue must consider him a monster about to pounce! He must control himself.

His teeth sank into the tip of his glove as he pulled it off, the sensation of the sliding leather caused his flesh to rebel.

His scars shone in the fire's glow. Most were patches of sunburst, others white arches dealt by the surgeon to remove the shrapnel.

Waterloo had taken too much from him.

They had been behind blockades, firing, trying to hold their position to stop Napoleon's men from breaking through.

One moment, he'd been shouting orders, blood staining his vision and his shako sliding over one eye, the next his musket backfired, pieces embedded in his hands.

Then the agony in the hospital tent, fever, the threat of losing his hands altogether.

In the end they had been spared but were so badly scarred he hid them so as not to frighten Imogen.

Tomorrow he would apologise to Virtue and then avoid her. She was too tempting. Too headstrong and curious — and exactly who he had wanted when he was a boy.

★ ★ ★

Virtue pushed the chest of drawers in front of her door. She sat upon the bed in her nightgown, knees tucked against her chest, her hair loose.

She needed to rest and the bed's silky sheets tempted her to surrender. But what might she wake to? She imagined August standing over her in a dragon's mask, raising a ceremonial dagger.

'My blasted imagination!' she seethed, throwing herself down.

She tried to find some other reason for him caressing her cheek — a stray lock of hair, a spider, anything accidental.

She wanted to see the best in him. If not, if she had to admit she was afraid, her only option would be to leave and that would be the end of her aspirations.

One who'd latch upon her failure was her father, who wanted a skivvy as replacement for her poor, overworked mother.

Virtue rolled on her side, watching a shadow of movement pass the slit under her door. She stiffened, but the person left.

She must remain. Nothing, neither rumours or truth, would chase her out.

Lord Winterton was simply a man. A father. A widower. Her childhood friend.

She had been shaken since Jeb had revealed his true intent but she would not curl inwards and ignore the world. She needed to live her life.

Sleep came, after an hour of thrashing.

The nightmares returned. She ran through tunnels looping into one another with no way out. The candle she clutched melted into nothing until her hands were sticky with wax.

Chasing her through this maze came the tapping scrape of some unknown creature's claws.

A Locked Garden

The next day a letter appeared beneath Virtue's door with a seal of pure black.

Miss Browne,

I ask forgiveness for my actions last night. Once again I have shown myself to be someone distasteful. I know it will frustrate you, yet I can only say I have my reasons but am unable to divulge them.

While you remain here I will take all measures not to impose upon you.

A. Winterton.

The words were shaky, as though he had written this with every bit of energy he had. She was both amused and annoyed. Did he blame her for his actions simply because she had sat too close or looked too inviting?

Mingled with relief was a sense of regret. There would be no more fireside talks.

August was not her concern. It was the mystery of him which stoked her curiosity, nothing more.

Imogen showed Virtue around the house once lessons were over. But when the governess pointed to a staircase at the side of the hall the girl clung to her skirt.

'We cannot go there!' she whispered, eyes wide. 'That is the west wing. I wanted to see Mother's room but Papa caught me. He was so . . . It's the only time he has raised his voice.'

Virtue squeezed her hand.

'Then we will find other entertainment.'

The view from one of those ruined rooms must be breathtaking, she mused. Think of standing there in a storm!

But, of course, it would not just be breathtaking, it would also be deadly.

They made their way outside. The gardens were enclosed, edged with topiary and crawling vines. Bracken jutted, entwined with roses mottled white in their centres.

At the front stood a single black gate, taller than any man and tipped with spikes.

Virtue glanced at the manor, wondering if the house really was swaying in the winds.

She saw Lord Winterton's silhouette through his study window, barely visible in the insipid gleam of daylight emerging between smudged clouds. He was pacing.

The gate was pushed open and Imogen smiled.

'Mr Charles!'

The man was the same age as Virtue's father, though his face was lined and ruddy with joy rather than weariness and overindulgence. He pulled off his floppy, wide-brimmed hat to wipe his forehead, revealing grey hair peppered white.

'Hello, there, little one.'

He bent low to speak to Imogen then straightened and turned to Virtue.

'Harold Charles, miss. I manage the stables and everything in the grounds.'

'May we go inside the gardens?'

The smile went and he sucked at his teeth.

'It's not safe. The sea's been biting here.'

Something in the way his stone-grey eyes held hers, keeping eye contact, made her suspicious.

He closed the gate and turned the key in the lock, tucking it into his ragged waistcoat pocket.

Once he left Virtue peered between the bars. She could make out a willow tree and the curved form of a statue draped in trailing leaves and shadows. For the briefest of seconds it seemed as if the stone shifted and the statue breathed.

Virtue shut her eyes, telling herself not to be ridiculous.

When she looked again she noticed, further in, some sort of opening in the ground. Perhaps the entrance to the rumoured tunnels?

Imogen was still annoyed she could not show off her garden.

'It's not fair! I walked through here yesterday. It was fine then! There is another way where the bushes are not so thick. Let's sneak in!'

Virtue was tempted to disregard Lord Winterton's orders. She knew this was childish, simply a way to rebel against him because his contradictory nature had left her frustrated and reeling.

'No,' she decided. 'Think how upset your father would be if you were hurt.

'I have some paints. We can draw the view from your window.'

They returned to the manor. On instinct, Virtue looked up.

She saw a ramrod figure with his arms behind his back. August had stopped pacing.

He stood looking out, watching them. Had he been anticipating her disobedience?

There were too many secrets in this household.

Tonight Virtue would find out for herself whether the waves had claimed the gardens.

On the Brink!

Virtue heard the ticking of a distant clock she had yet to find. Eleven strikes sounded.

Her candle flickered on the window-sill as she peered outside. This was foolishness. She risked possible harm and the ire of her employer just to hush her inquisitiveness.

But to be kept in the dark always irritated Virtue. Here at Winterton Manor every room held a secret.

She left her room and went to the kitchens, exiting via the servant's entrance.

Gusts ruffled the grasses and her dress as she stepped outside. The moon was not there to guide her.

She heard a screech as the gate opened and shut, buffeted by sea winds. She held it still, wincing at the whine it made, then slipped in and shut it behind her.

The crash of waves roared somewhere below and a gull battled with the elements.

The light from her candle only suggested what lay beyond. She might easily take a wrong step and tumble to her death.

Her eyes streamed and her cheeks stung from the cold. The tight confines of her braid could not withstand the probing wind. Lock after lock came loose.

Virtue wanted to run to bed and pretend this was another nightmare to join the others plaguing her. But she had already risked much and would not allow herself the weakness of slinking inside.

She went to where she knew the willow tree and statue stood, her hand outstretched until she felt the hard stone. She lifted the candle to see better.

The statue was of a mermaid, head turned aside shyly and tail tucked to her chest. Time and rain had eroded the features into empty smoothness.

The willow's long leaves curled around the mermaid's tail, skittering and getting trapped. At least Virtue knew what had made her think the statue had moved.

Roses and lilies crumbled softly

beneath her shoes as she felt her way. The toe of her boot carefully pressed down as she searched for stable ground but the flowers tricked her into thinking the ground was too soft and liable to come apart.

Her candle blew out and in that same moment Virtue's footing went, the earth under her crumbling into nothingness.

She wheeled desperately to regain her balance, a cry for help knotted in her throat. No-one would know she had vanished.

She would fall, to be swallowed by the sea and forgotten.

She teetered, her heel stamping behind, her blood racing. She'd stopped herself from falling. She was safe.

Warmth encircled her waist. Someone had helped her. A man.

'Lord Winterton!' she said, breathless. There was no response.

She made to face him but his hold tightened, forcing her to stare at the abyss below. The waves had paled to a crystalline colour. Foam white as bone swept across as effortlessly as a hand gesture.

Barely any of the beach remained, the pale sands glowing harshly. Another statue lay in pieces and was claimed by the sea.

Virtue wavered on the edge, her survival reliant on another's benevolence. She shook, then felt anger as she felt on her neck the man's hot breath, tinged sweet with whisky.

'Let me go,' Virtue demanded.

After a long pause which caused her heart to race again she was turned to face him.

'Jeb. Why are you here?'

So it had been Jeb who had left open the gate for her to slip through. He must have been watching her stumble in the darkness.

She held back a shudder. He must not see her fear.

Foolish Girl!

Jeb's eyes were bloodshot and his whiskers a little longer and darker than before. His scarred chin stood out clearly.

His smile was the same as when they were children, yet it had never frightened her then. She had always believed, no matter what, he would never harm her.

'I'm out wandering, just as I always am,' he answered, his voice rough.

'You must leave! Lord Winterton would not want you here.'

'What about you?'

He pulled her closer.

'Did August asked you to meet him here? Silly girl, you should have kept to your warm bedroom. He wouldn't have argued.'

She made to kick, furious at what he suggested, but behind her she felt only emptiness and wind. It was either fall or remain in his arms.

He chuckled, pressing his cheek to hers.

'Don't worry, I'll not let you go,' he whispered. 'I'd never hurt you without reason, Virtue. Come, don't purse your lips. I like it when you smile.

'I'm sorry for betting you. I should have known you wouldn't see the joke.'

'I am not some gin-woman plying her trade! I was your friend!'

This man had been her first kiss, perhaps even her first love.

'Well, you've hit me and you've shouted, now calm yourself.'

He pulled a blue ribbon from his jacket.

'This'll cheer you; a nice pretty ribbon.'

His fingers gripped her hair to tie it up. He was so broad she felt smothered.

'Jeb.' She spoke softly, trying one last time. 'Let me go back inside.'

'I want a thank you for my gift,' he growled, breathing heavily.

Then she heard a dog snarl and felt relief.

'Here!' she called, choking as Jeb's hand dragged over her mouth.

'Look what you've done!' he hissed, shaking her. 'Why did you always trust him more than me?'

'Get your hands off her!' August ordered. 'I'll flay your hide if you remain on my property a moment longer.'

His riding boots glimmered with seawater. His dogs circled him, bodies hunched, ready to spring upon his command.

Jeb thrust her aside and for a terrifying moment she feared she had been flung over the edge. She thought she heard Lord Winterton cry out.

Instead she fell upon the grass, her arm splayed over the mermaid statue's tail.

'Jebediah Strawhouse.' Lord Winterton faced the man. 'Just the prey I hoped for. I'll see you swing for what you've done.'

'And I'll drag you down with me, you sanctimonious runt!'

Jeb lunged for August who moved aside. The innkeeper gripped the back of his cape and wrenched him off balance.

Dogs howled, snapping at the tussling pair.

August struck out with his foot, connecting with Jeb's knee.

Virtue could not lay there and watch them half-kill one another. She threw herself between them.

'Stop this at once!'

Blood smeared August's cheek from where Jeb had clawed at him. Jeb had the upper hand, fingers clenched tight around Lord Winterton's throat.

'All of it should have been mine,' Jeb snarled. 'Her as well!'

His face twisted in agony and fury, August shakily made a fist and struck out with all his might at Jeb's face. With a wail of pain Jeb released August, falling back and clutching his nose.

He made to lunge again.

Virtue only had one way of stopping him. She wrapped herself around August. Jeb would have to drag her off to get to him.

'Leave now!' she shouted, voice shaky.

The dogs turned to Jeb, their lips

pulled back to show off their teeth. He ran and they chased him, barking into the night.

Only then did Virtue relax, a great weariness crawling through every limb.

She panted, dangerously close to sobbing but holding herself in check.

She knew how easily she might have fallen and perished. A single thing done differently could have been the end of her.

She felt a gentle touch to her hip and started, remembering who it was she clumsily embraced.

Virtue flung herself away.

'I am so sorry, Lord Winterton!'

She watched, still and quiet like a frightened animal, as August faced her.

Colour had fled his face save for his lips and his right hand was tucked under his coat.

'Go back inside,' he told her harshly, causing her to flinch. 'I'll not stay up half the night because some foolish girl had her assignation ruined!'

He stormed off in the direction of the

manor before her shock could dissolve into anger.

For the final time this night the gate squealed as it was opened and shut.

Give Me Your Hand

August strode through the corridor to the library. There he ducked beneath a curtain and sat upon the window-sill.

He tore his gloves off, grimacing at what was revealed. His hands had turned an angry colour from the skin being stretched. They looked and felt as though afire.

He had held back his discomfort but it was too late now. The pain had caught hold and nothing could sway it until it decided to pass.

His eyes shut and he calmed his breathing, willing the licking flames to soften.

He should have left the house armed — he knew how dangerous the land hereabouts had become. But he had not expected someone to dare sneak on to his property!

His grimace deepened. Jebediah Strawhouse had become a troublesome thorn; he'd do well to prune him out of his life.

Why had Virtue been out there? He'd thought her a sensible creature yet her actions proved otherwise.

Her involvement with Jeb would lead her to an early grave or, worse, marriage. Surely Jeb's treatment of her in the inn would have put her off the rat?

It had been the same all those years ago, the other boy snatching Virtue's hand from August's and dragging her elsewhere.

And she had always let him do it.

The library door opened and August, partially concealed by the damask curtain, pressed his mouth to his split knuckles as he saw Virtue.

She glanced around, searching for him, but he remained where he was.

Most women would have calmed themselves by trying to tame the wildness of their hair. Miss Browne's was still windswept and dripping wet with sea spray.

A gaudy ribbon hung from one damp lock. She shook it out, letting it fall.

Removing a well-used volume about Breton folktales from the shelf she walked towards him. August tensed, uncertain how much of his shadow could be seen.

The book held her attention as Virtue sat in the chair by his window-sill. She wore no gloves and a small, tanned finger crooked under the corner of each page to turn it.

August, holding his breath, did not move from where he hid. He could hear her own ragged breathing.

Her cheek was tense from withheld anger and the rest of her body thrummed.

Then he noticed her hands were shaking.

She clasped them as if to hide her nerves, anger making way for anxious energy.

There was plenty for Virtue to tremble over tonight.

August could not understand her attraction to Jeb. He was a violent man and none could change his ways. In his shifting moods he turned on any woman who tried to claim him.

When August had come across the pair he had only meant to chase Jeb off. He had not realised how close they were to peril.

If Jeb had thrown Virtue aside any harder she would have been over the edge before August had a chance to catch her.

He was aghast as he remembered seeing her hair stream behind her, hands blindly thrust out to stop her fall.

Now he noticed, staining her blouse, a trickle of his own blood from the wound upon his head. He no longer felt the cold of the night he had escaped.

He did not even realise his pain had dulled, distracted by this woman who was both friend and stranger.

August might have considered her lost to Jeb entirely were it not for her actions — she had shielded him from further harm. He still felt the beat of her pulse upon his cheek.

As though she sensed his thoughts Virtue's head slowly lifted. Her shadow went still.

He half-held his breath, knowing he

could not escape this confrontation as her hand reached out and pulled aside the curtain.

He almost enjoyed seeing the way her mouth fell open in shock, eyes wide, yet her eyebrows furrowed in annoyance.

'Lord Winterton!'

His gloves! Where were they? No longer were they cradled on his lap.

He pulled his wretched hands to himself and hid them within his coat, hoping Virtue had yet to notice.

Seeing her, August found the last of his anger abating. He would not allow himself to take his frustrations out on Virtue because of his hatred for Jeb.

'Forgive me for my earlier words.' He smiled wryly.

It seemed he had to apologise to her at least once a day.

'I did not expect to find Strawhouse there. So long as you live in my house he is barred from here. He is someone I do not want Imogen to encounter.'

She frowned as though she would like to argue, then nodded wearily.

'I promise he will not come here again.'

He was surprised she gave up so easily but she had another preoccupation.

'Let me tend your wounds. You're bleeding.' She produced a handkerchief which was soon stained with the red of his blood.

'Thank you,' he murmured gruffly, hunching in on himself.

Her scent washed over him. She smelt of rain and winds alongside the calm of lavender. His eyelids slowly fell, close to shutting as he leaned into her warmth.

Virtue removed the handkerchief from his forehead and assessed him.

'You were hurt elsewhere. Give me your hands.'

Not waiting, she snatched for one before asking why he concealed them.

As her fingers curled around his wrist he knew she felt the rough, burning flesh and saw the way his face twisted.

Her touch was cool, soft but firm. Her lips pursed in confusion as she pulled his hand into view.

August could not stand to see that

confusion harden into disgust or, worse, melt into pity. He could not face the humiliation.

He shook off her gentle, unbearable caresses and all but ran out of the library.

He must lock himself away in his room. No sensible woman would dare follow him there.

The Letter

Virtue was left behind in the library. Stunned, she clutched her bloodied handkerchief.

Lord Winterton had run from her as if she were a rabid dog. Someone such as he, who a short while earlier had threatened to flay Jeb alive, was frightened of her!

Virtue struggled to comprehend, yet recalled his look of disgust and dread. Something had turned the furrow of his brow, like a chisel, to stone.

His face was pale and his eyes bright . . . August was in pain. Why?

He had run from her when she touched his hands so it must be them. She tried to recall the brief glimpse she'd had of them and how they had felt in hers.

Her first thought was that his hands were incredibly broad, easily engulfing hers. They were bare of any hairs, with the roughness of an unfamiliar texture.

She had felt the jut of his bones in his

73

wrist and seen how his hands tapered at the ends into long, delicate fingers.

He had scars, she realised. Skin blistered in places and angry puckers where wounds had tried to heal in all manner of ways.

As she tugged on her own gloves Virtue wondered how desperately a man must hate his hands to hide them always.

To be afraid of baring ones flesh must be an anxious, frustrating existence.

She did not retreat to her room. From her wanderings with Imogen she had guessed where August slept and she made her way there.

She hesitated, her fingers curled to knock. What would it look like if one of the servants were to come upon this? This was not a governess's duty.

But Virtue had never been a coward. August would do well to remember how reckless she could be.

'Lord Winterton?' She rapped against the wood. 'Please, August, come out.'

She waited but the door did not open. She heard only the shaky drag of her own breathing.

'I did not properly see your hands, my Lord, but I know they pain you. You do not have to struggle alone.

'Let me be your friend again.'

Virtue tried opening the door herself but it would not move. She imagined him standing on the other side, gripping the handle to stop her.

Frustration won out.

'Why must men bottle up their pain?

There is nothing strong about suffering in silence.

'The only thing pitiful is how you shut yourself away!'

Virtue walked away from the bedroom door. She leaned against the corridor wall, the flush on her face cooling.

She should not have been confrontational. It would only rouse his pride.

Anger was of no use here but it was proof of how much he affected her. And he did, very much so, even if she could not understand why.

For one absurd moment she imagined ramming the door to rescue the man from himself. But she knew she would merely bounce off the wood.

She would not let the matter rest. If August was mulish enough to ignore her she must inundate him with persuasion.

Virtue left a letter for him in the library.

Dear Lord Winterton,

I was disappointed by your departure tonight. For someone who apparently takes pride in shocking society with his outlandish behaviour you are very quick to excuse yourself when such behaviour arises.

I do not want you to suffer in silence. There are many years of your life left. Do not taint them.

Find joy in your daughter, your home, your friends. Please consider me one of them once more.

I will assist you in whatever way you demand. All you need do is ask.

Together I am certain we can find a way to overcome this.

August might throw this on the fire without reading it. After all, most men would be furious at being told what to do by a woman.

She hoped August's progressive ideas were his true beliefs.

P.S. I know you are upset about Jeb Strawhouse, August. I must protest my innocence. I did not invite him.

Even if you will not accept my help, are you not curious as to why he was there?

★ ★ ★

August could not remain in his room for the rest of the year. It wasn't as if a tiger stalked his corridors, merely a slight thing of a woman.

Though perhaps the truly dangerous creature was the one without stripes and claws . . .

He opened the door, tense, almost expecting the governess to leap from a shadowed corner, pin him and demand the answers he kept from her. But the corridor was empty. No tigresses were roaming.

He relaxed in relief and disappointment.

His gloves were still in the library. With his fingers curled and arms stiffly held from having his hands exposed, he returned to where he had run from.

August's gut lurched to think of himself as a coward. In the Army he had never shirked his duty nor turned down a challenge.

Since his injury he'd avoided society. Others could not withstand the shadows and silence of the manor. In the end, everyone left him alone.

Virtue's stubbornness would be refreshing if it wasn't such a hindrance to his solitude.

He found his gloves tucked beneath her letter. No doubt there was condemnation within. Smiling thinly, he found a letter opener.

An object glistened on the floor, caught in the firelight. August crouched and saw it was the ribbon. Jeb Strawhouse's gift.

A sneer curled his lips as he lifted the thing with his knife and flicked the offending article into the blaze.

It was as tacky as the man who had chosen it. Its gaudy colour would clash with the governess's hair — as if attention should be diverted from those dark tresses.

Had August been the one to give her such a gift it would have been burgundy. The colour would accentuate the slightly curling locks, inviting a person to run their fingers through them.

August opened the letter and slowly read through what she had to say.

So she wished to challenge him into accepting her help? A part of him flared, proudly claiming he needed no-one's assistance.

But he also felt great shame over his condition.

There was no disgust in this letter, only honesty and concern and something else he could not name.

Together I am certain we can find a way to overcome this.

His thumb passed over the words.

He was Lord Winterton, an ex-soldier,

a father. Someone even considered a folktale monster by others.

It had been a long time since he had simply been August. He had locked away his wants ever since Imogen had been thrust into his life.

Let her take on the challenge, if Virtue was as willing as she made out.

He would show her the rumoured tunnels and what lay within.

Imogen's Wild Mother

The sea was calm. Waves stroked across damp sands and a single gull bobbed, regal and poised, going wherever the sea fancied.

Dune grasses shivered as dawn arrived and light pierced the water. The gull ruffled its feathers as warmth pervaded its wings.

Virtue arose early, her head in a fugue as though last night had not truly ended.

She walked along the outer edges of the gardens. It looked different in the daylight, faded and crouched in on itself. The roses were turning papery and discoloured.

A dog lay stretched out before the gate which now held a second lock. Mr Charles was trimming the hedges with shears.

She watched until he noticed her.

'The master's been telling me what you did last night. It was very foolish.

'You be careful by the dunes, girl.

They ferry off the ones with too much spirit but not enough sense,' he added.

'Yes, well . . .' She floundered over what to say then settled on her first instinct, which was rudeness. 'I did not ask for your opinion.'

'You did not, nor did I ask for your permission to speak. Too much like her, that's what you are.'

He resumed his work. The dog's tail thumped in lazy annoyance at a fly.

'Who am I like?'

He went on tiptoe to reach one particular piece of foliage, cheeks puffing red from the effort.

'The last lady of the house. Chastity, Imogen's mother.'

'Lord Winterton's wife?'

Mr Charles went silent, examining the claws of the bracken. Sweat glimmered on his forehead.

'What was she like?'

'Oh, so now you want to hear my voice?'

Virtue flushed.

'I'm sorry I was sharp. I had hoped the

incident would remain between myself and August — Lord Winterton.'

Mr Charles grunted.

'Chastity looks nothing like you, if that's what you're wondering. A good thing, too. She was wild. It drives people to want to subdue such a spirit.'

'How did she die?'

'It was after she gave birth. Those injuries were too much for her. They would be for anyone.'

Whistling, he left her standing there. The dog remained, ears flicking at the sound of her breath turning ragged.

She was puzzled. The way the gardener had spoken of Chastity Winterton's death it was as if her wounds had not been inflicted by childbirth but by another.

* * *

Mr Charles's comments remained with Virtue throughout the day. While Imogen jabbed her quill pen into her inkpot, Virtue watched and wondered.

She tried to picture the girl's mother.

83

The woman she imagined was an elegant creature, thin but with rosy cheeks, full smiling lips and trails of thick, pale hair curling around her.

Impetuous. Mischievous.

She considered whether Imogen's personality was a watery reflection of the mother's. Virtue believed in nurture rather than nature.

It would be Lord Winterton's dark humour merged with Lady Winterton's looks. A powerful combination.

When they paused for tea and lemon cakes that Cook had sent up, Virtue probed gently.

'Does your father speak about your mother?'

Imogen cut her cake slowly into uniform square pieces.

'I have to beg him to. Once, he told me she was like a mermaid. She loved swimming and wandering the beach at night.'

She began crumbling the cake pieces with her fingers, frowning.

Virtue pressed her lips together,

cursing her curiosity. She had gone too far.

'Imogen, I'm sorry —'

A door slammed overhead. Heavy footsteps strode over and a chair scraped.

Governess and student both approached the open window.

Lord Winterton could be heard, though his voice was a murmur. His visitor, however, boomed his responses.

'We're ready, August.'

Imogen quickly hissed to Virtue that the voice belonged to William Matthews, the local Customs and Excise officer.

He often came to see her father when he headed the Assizes.

'My men spied them offloading cargo from the ship and harvesting their crops from the sea.

'The only place they could have taken them to is the Retreat. We'll get them this time.'

Virtue shivered as a cool breeze blew past. The grainy impression of sea salt felt thick enough to lick from her lips.

'The patrons are sure to rebel but we'll haul them to the custom house if we have to.'

Lord Winterton must have realised suddenly how unguarded their conversation was, for the study windows were slammed shut.

A lump of stone seemed lodged in Virtue's throat and gooseflesh ran up her arms.

They were going to raid the Seagull's Retreat! Whatever Jeb was involved in she did not care about, but her father would be there.

If he became embroiled in this, he would try to argue and the officers might strike him. As much as her father blustered and raged he was an old man.

She must warn him.

'Imogen,' she said hurriedly, afraid there would not be enough time, 'I must leave for the village.'

'We could ask Mr Charles for a horse,' the girl offered. 'Mine is tame enough if you are not used to riding.'

'No, I'll walk. Thank you, though.'

She could not have anyone knowing what she planned. Everyone here belonged to Lord Winterton — including her, in a way.

Warning!

Virtue hurried to her room, changed into walking boots and put on her cloak, raising the hood as she left.

She walked while in sight of the manor, but once she could not feel the looming breadth of its shadow she ran.

It was a mile to the inn. Virtue hurried over the water-drenched sands which slurped at her boots.

Minuscule grains flew into her face, like rat claws scoring over her cheeks. Her breath rasped and she flinched as the wind roared, a high-pitched screeching noise piercing her eardrums.

So much effort did it take yet it seemed she made no progress. The only way she could tell it was not hopeless was by sight of the approaching dunes.

Virtue looked up, eyes squinting from the grit. There it was, the sign. She had arrived at the Seagull's Retreat.

She climbed the small hill, her legs shaking from the effort, and almost fell through the doorway of the inn.

Shuck was licking a woman's fingers as she offered him some of her meal. The young man who had served last time stood smoking with a friend.

All was peaceful. Customs and Excise had yet to appear.

Jeb was manning the bar. Virtue pulled her hood closer and went to the rooms upstairs. She knocked on her father's door. He was not inside.

An old woman emerged from another room, stained bedsheets tucked in her arms. She glanced at Virtue dully.

'Is my father still here?'

'He's in the cellar,' she told her. 'He couldn't pay his tab so we set him some things to do.'

Virtue hurried downstairs. She hovered in the shadows, watching the bar.

When a group of fishermen came in, stinking of brine, sopping wet and swearing at one another, Jeb carried over several tankards.

Virtue darted into the back room and hurried to the cellar.

'Father?'

It was dark inside. A candle flickered high in its holder but its light kept close to itself.

Slowly, Virtue's eyes adjusted as she carefully went down the steps.

The air was muggy from permeating damp. She made her way around rows of barrels which covered the ground.

'Father!' she called again. 'You must leave with me now!'

Bottles had been slotted into racks carved in the stone walls. Something dark jumped from one bottle neck to the other.

Someone was rummaging about with a barrel, humming under his breath. The water he poured lightened the dark colour of the brandy.

There was a slit oilskin bag of tobacco sat alongside a bowl of ashes and wood shavings.

'You're adulterating?' she asked her father in disbelief.

Tobacco and brandy. She knew what this meant: smuggling. The punishment was either hanging or transportation.

If her father was found tampering with the contraband . . .

'It is to weaken it, my child. Those who drink this will not become as intoxicated as they would have been otherwise.'

He chuckled.

'And it's the best way to make a profit.'

'We have to go! Customs will —'

Her elbow was gripped from behind.

'Customs will what?' Jeb hissed.

Blood stained through the bandages over his nose.

'My life depends on this, Virtue. Speak.'

The Smuggler's Way

Jeb shook her harshly. She looked to her father who frowned.

'Tell him, girl, this is important. None of your hysterics.'

'This man is a villain, Father. He tried to — he has tried to harm me!'

'With a tongue like yours is it any surprise?' Jeb replied cheerfully. 'You know how trying you can be, Virtue, and you take jests in all the wrong ways.

'Now, tell me what you came to say.'

She did not want to help Jeb but once Customs came they would find her and her father. Everyone, including Lord Winterton, would assume she was involved.

'They're coming to raid this place.'

Cursing, Jeb hollered the names of his men. Three appeared and he ordered them to lift the barrels.

Virtue's father hurried to stuff the tobacco back into its bag, careful not to spill any.

Pulling Virtue along with him Jeb went towards one of the racks. He jerked a bottle and the wall dragged open to reveal a cuddy. The barrels were placed inside.

'Keep an eye out and make sure she doesn't give us up.'

He thrust her in and her father followed. The false wall inched shut.

Above, someone pounded on the door. A commanding voice boomed for everyone to remain seated.

The false wall settled in place just as footsteps entered the cellar. Virtue was left in utter darkness.

She pressed her hands against damp stones crawling with moss. The barrels crowded around her. It was too small, too dark. There wasn't enough air!

'Father!'

'Hush!' His hand clamped over her mouth. Only when she scratched at his wrist did he let her breathe.

'Why are you doing this?' Her face was wet. 'This is wrong!'

'It is the way. When you were a girl I

stored things for smugglers in the school-house. How do you think your mother could keep wearing silk and you reading your books?'

The books she had had to abandon when he set out on his missionary work.

Perhaps her stolen kiss with Jeb had not been the cause of their leaving here. Her father might have been escaping prison if Customs had started to suspect.

'You would not have become a governess without me allowing you to study. You can be independent of me,' he went on bitterly, 'but how else am I to pay for food and board?'

'And your drink,' she wanted to snap. 'I thought you disapproved of Jeb and his father,' she said instead.

On the other side of the wall Jeb was inviting the Customs man to have a drink. The response he got was the cellar door slamming shut. He had got away with it.

'Tom Strawhouse was always running his mouth and the deluded boy believed he was better than us. Now, he's started being sensible. You'd benefit if you helped us.'

'How?'

'As you did today. All you need do is listen and let us know if you hear anything concerning our activities.'

'And betray my employer?'

'You don't owe that man any loyalty.'

Before she could retort the false wall heaved open. She darted out as soon as the gap was wide enough, crawling over Jeb's sand-encrusted boots.

She shakily heaved herself to her feet and he stepped back, grinning.

'They never even realised. It was good of you to warn me.'

Jeb reached into his apron and removed a money pouch. He took her hand and prised her fingers open, placing it there.

'There's more where that came from, if you . . .'

'Never!'

She rushed out of the inn and into the fresh air. Her father followed.

'I should have left you to suffer the consequences!' she cried.

'And abandon your father? No true daughter would do that.'

He was right that he was all she had, but she would never help smugglers.

Virtue thrust the money pouch at him.

'Take this and leave. There must be a school out there that will take you.'

He stared at the money, then smiled.

'You always knew how to look after your father. I'll get my things.'

Virtue sank down upon a rock and wrapped her arms around herself.

Her eyes were sore. Wetness gleamed at the corners.

Why did she persist in going to her father's aid? There was never gratitude or kindness. Each time she saved him he promised to change. Always, it was thrown in her face.

If she could not trust her father, how could she trust any other man?

Sharp caws sounded overhead. Crows forewarning the ending day like a blanket of night about to fall.

Virtue dabbed at her eyes and cheeks. It was no use wasting her tears.

She needed to return to Winterton Manor.

* ★ ★

One of Matthews's men had just left, grim-faced, having brought a report on tonight's raid.

August thrust open the study windows, baring his face to the fluttering cool winds.

Light vanished behind the dunes, the sky opaque and dark as though replaced by the sea. Crows were flying, dark ink spots replacing gull white.

Instead of Napoleon's soldiers August now pitted himself against a worse enemy: the greed of the smuggler.

Customs and Excise men were found beaten, shot or hanged, with little mercy shown, over some barrels of gin and brandy. Men were worth less than profit.

Whenever August thought he had the evidence needed it was snatched away. Each time Strawhouse was dragged to trial witnesses vanished or others of far higher rank vouched for him.

August had hoped to be rid of Jeb by just and legal means. As his options lessened, however, he feared he would have to resort to the same unsavoury methods as the smuggler.

Jeb was the main reason August could not completely trust Virtue. Her loyalties were divided. She might be a trap.

And that was why, as he looked down from the window, he considered this the machinations of fate.

Virtue was running towards the manor. Her cloak billowed and she heaved with effort yet seemed to be hunched in on herself, no doubt desperate not to be seen.

He should have realised from the start that she had become embroiled with Strawhouse!

August now knew why the report from his man would be unsuccessful. Virtue had been in her lover's ear, warning him.

He stepped away from the window. Let her think he remained ignorant of her deception.

Virtue's letter went the same place as Jeb's ribbon. The paper curled in on itself, fire creeping over her words.

August watched the flames, something bright hot burning in his chest as well.

Mercy and honesty were not the weapons to use against smugglers. Their language was violence and trickery.

It was time for August to counter-attack.

Inside the Tunnels

Virtue hurried up the steps of the manor. She had not meant to be out for so long. How could she possibly explain this?

She had foiled a Customs and Excise investigation. For all she knew she had bungled months of planning!

A shadow moved by one of the snarling wyvern statues.

'You have a habit of wandering about at night, Virtue,' Lord Winterton announced. 'You must take care lest you encounter something unpleasant.'

The only thing she could discern was his voice. He was hidden in the darkness while she was caught in a shard of moonlight.

She only hoped he would not mistake her shiver for trembling.

'I went to the village.' It was not quite a lie. 'I had some business with my father to deal with. I'm sorry.'

'I was worried for you, especially after last night.' Steps sounded as he came closer. 'I thought it best to give my response to your letter in person.'

'And your answer?' Her voice was quiet and he drew even nearer to hear better.

'You will do whatever I command?'

She tried to gauge the tone of his voice. It held an edge, like a creature anticipating whether to bite.

'Within reason.'

'So already you are backtracking?'

She was never one to retreat.

'Not at all. Tell me what it is you want.'

Lord Winterton stepped into the light.

'Come with me to the tunnels. See what I hide there, then you'll understand.'

He did not wait for her response. Grasping her arm he led her to the gardens.

The dog standing guard was dismissed with a command. August unlocked the gate which screamed as he thrust it open.

The tunnel entrance looked nothing more than a black hole.

Inside, cloying damp greeted them

101

along with salt and the muggy scent of seaweed.

As August pulled her along she recalled today's lesson with Imogen — Hades carrying Persephone to the Underworld.

But there would be no Demeter to rage and demand her return.

'Are you warm enough?' he asked. 'It can be as cold as bare bones here.'

He draped his cloak over hers as an extra layer and they went into the darkness.

A tiny flicker of light winked, then grew, revealing a lantern set in place.

'Generations of my family have dug their way into these dunes,' he told her. 'There were tunnels before these ones, hiding places for Viking gold or barrows holding the bones of pagans.

'Some run as far as the village, others even further. Still more are collapsed and are nothing more than a tomb.

'This will be your tomb if you stray from my side,' he added.

He released her, taking the lantern. Instinct told Virtue not to go any further though her curiosity hungered for more.

Stories of spirits had always entranced her. Under the hot sun of her travels, where daily danger was real, they seemed distant.

These tunnels made her think differently. Here were many paths, as twisted as a sailor's knot.

She tried to take note of which way to go should she need to escape, yet could not.

'Do you really want to know what goes on in here?' August whispered in her ear.

He reached for her hand and clasped it. The rough texture of leather scraped over the softness of her woollen gloves.

Shadows passed, dancing in their light. She imagined incense smoke, robes embroidered with arcane symbols and blood streaked on the ground in the dreaded sign of evil . . .

But the sand was damp and untouched.

The walls were bare.

A figure emerged, hand reaching for her. August raised the lantern to reveal a statue of a young man with the legs of a goat — a satyr from Greek mythology.

She freed herself from August's hold to better examine it.

'Why is it here?' Why hidden away?

'When I was young, to my father's horror I wanted to be an artist. Pencils, oils, clay, stone. Anything I could get my hands on.'

She remembered once, while playing with Jeb, she'd called for August to join them. He had shaken his head.

Too engrossed with a book, she had thought, only to peer over his shoulder and discover he had been sketching her.

'My father was a hard man,' he continued. 'I suppose I am spiting him by covering my gardens and walls with beauty.

'It is all I can do now. Since my injury I find it difficult to draw for long periods of time. I still yearn for it, though.'

He tilted her head.

'I am sorry I frightened you before. You captured my interest. I hid my work thinking I could forget, but I cannot.

'That is my reason for bringing you here.'

They went further in, the tunnel expanding to resemble a small room.

There were figures of stags and wolves, cherubs and goddesses. In the centre of the room tools had been abandoned next to a single block of stone and a chair.

'I want you to pose for me,' he told her.

'As what?'

'Woman, Virtue. Pygmalion's statue.'

'Absolutely not!' She was horrified. 'I will not display myself as . . .'

She waved towards a statue of a nymph.

'I cannot! I will not.'

'Of course I would not ask you to pose in such a way.' His lips quirked. 'All you need do is sit. Will you deny me this request?'

'Are you blackmailing me, sir?'

He leaned forward, eyes dark.

'No, my dear. I am daring you.'

Clearly he hungered for something. Virtue could not tell what it was but, if she did this for him, she might learn.

She wanted to discover everything. His wounds. Little Imogen and her mother.

Why August kept himself hidden in the manor while everyone thought him a frightening folk legend.

This was a dangerous game, however. Would her reward be satisfaction for feeding her curiosity, or might she feel the fangs of a beast?

The West Wing

The next day mirrored Virtue's mood. Bushes were dragged this way and that in the gusts. Tiny stones rattled and were dashed from the path.

The winds snarled and hissed, and the house groaned in response.

The only noise she could hear were her footsteps yet the back of her neck scrabbled with the sensation of being watched.

Virtue's thoughts returned to the tunnels. The statues frozen in the cold grip of stone. Her promise to return and be sculpted.

She glanced over her shoulder, but only saw shadows. Unable to stand it any longer she rushed to the refuge of her room.

A package lay upon her pillow. She pulled away the wrapping and a ribbon fluttered on to her lap, reminding her of Jeb's gift.

Who had left this for her? No doubt

Imogen, wanting to be kind.

The ribbon was slightly darker than her own hair yet not so apparent it appeared as if she was trying to seek attention. She knotted it at the base of her bun.

Her fears were foolish. It was only the manor's size and emptiness unnerving her.

Virtue made for the door. She would thank Imogen for the gift.

The girl's lively company would soon chase off any lingering doubts.

But Imogen could not be found in the library or classroom, nor even roaming the outskirts of the locked gardens.

As Virtue passed the stairs to the west wing a door banged shut. Her head jerked, hoping she was mistaken.

The wing was forbidden. Whatever Lord Winterton hid there was to stay a secret.

In her mind's eye she saw the yearning in Imogen's face. She had wanted to see her mother's room. It might be the only time she disobeyed her father.

A crack of thunder snapped and

Virtue jumped. The wing was not safe. Never mind protecting the child from her father's wrath, her very life might be at stake!

She bounded upstairs. What she stepped on to made her gasp. The corridor led to nothing. Broken apart, it revealed the outside.

She heard the crashing waves.

'Imogen!'

Her head spun; everything seeming to tilt.

The bedroom door halfway along jammed and she had to force her way through.

The room's roof had been whipped off, the walls broken in places. It was as though she stood within a shattered shell.

Water glimmered on everything and frigid rain drummed on her face.

Her eyes flicked about, her heart racing as she hunted for the girl.

Then she gasped.

Someone was there, opposite her. Not a child, or Jeb sneaking about, but a woman.

The woman stared without blinking. Green eyes shone bright, lips a deep red and, even in this tumult, parted as though to laugh.

She was as still as one of August's statues.

Something lodged itself in Virtue's throat. The woman's skin held no vitality, but was instead pale and cracked with an uneven, waxy hue.

Afraid the apparition would move before she did, Virtue stepped forward and her foot went through the rain-slicked floorboards.

Her screech was consumed by the next roar of thunder.

Wreckage shattered and darkness coated everything. Pain shot up Virtue's leg and shadows seeped into her eyes.

Where is She?

'Papa, wake up!'

August started, his head lifted from where it had been cushioned upon his desk.

He must have dozed, finally giving into fatigue. Since being in the tunnels he had not slept, his mind overwhelmed by sketches his hands could not keep up with.

'What is wrong, my dear?'

'Miss Browne did not come for evening class,' Imogen fretted.

'Perhaps she came over ill and retired to her room,' he reasoned.

Secretly he had a dark suspicion Virtue had slunk off to collude with Jeb.

'I looked. Her bed is empty!'

'You went in without permission? Your teacher deserves some privacy.'

'But where is she?' Imogen wailed. 'She would not have missed a lesson. We were discussing Mary Anning's sketches!'

Before she could dissolve into tears

111

August held open his arms. He bit down on his pain as she rocketed into his embrace.

'Do not fret,' he said against her curls. 'I'll search for her. Now, go ask Cook if she has anything sweet in need of eating.'

Imogen nodded jerkily then left.

August leaned back, stretching his legs and considering.

He was concerned for Virtue. No matter his contempt for her companions he knew the young woman would never miss a lesson, especially one concerning fossils.

He wondered if she had found the present he left on her bed. How hypocritical he had been to reprimand Imogen!

It had been another way of wooing Virtue. He had meant to give it to her in person yet had faltered over what to say, feeling like a shy boy once more.

Knowing Virtue, she would have hammered on his door rather than take off in fright.

August shrugged on his coat. He hadn't expected to be hunting a governess today.

He searched the house. Each time he found another room empty the churning in his gut spun faster. He needed to find her.

He stilled at the stairway leading to Chastity's bedchamber. Always, he kept his head bowed when passing this way, in shame and sorrow.

He would be glad when the sea finally claimed the west wing.

Today August forced himself to look. He frowned. He knew he had locked the door. Now it stood open.

Surely the woman had not been so foolish? Yet she might be if Jeb had been whispering in her ear and stoking her curiosity.

August mounted the steps and shoved the door open. Brittle winds scraped his face.

'Miss Browne — Virtue!'

He swallowed down panic at the thought of her tumbling beyond the corridor which was disintegrating into nothingness.

Lightning flickered quickly. Thunder

boomed as powerfully as the cannon fire which haunted his dreams.

Flashes of Chastity's room came upon him: the torn-apart bed; the family portrait ruined; a single, festering riding boot slumped on its side. August had to stop himself just before he pitched through the gaping chasm in the centre.

He clung to the edge, teeth gritted. Below, a woman's skirt fluttered in the gloom. Virtue lay on her side, curled up.

He called her name and, thank goodness, she stirred.

Another powerful gust shook the building. He must move fast. August went to the four-poster bed and tore up what remained of the curtains and bedspread, knotting the least rotted parts into rope.

Agony strummed the muscles of his hands but his own pain did not matter. He was stronger than his flesh.

Carefully, August lowered himself down till he crouched beside Virtue.

Her eyes opened, clouded in confusion. Before she could panic he clapped his stinging hands. Their gazes locked.

'Come,' he commanded, giving her no chance to disobey. 'We must leave. Put your arms around me.'

She did so. Her frigid cheek pressed against his as she clung to him, curls of her loose hair curving over his chin.

'Hold on.'

August gripped the rope and heaved them up. Virtue's breathing pattered against his own pounding pulse. Sweat streaked his face, turned icy in an instant by the winds.

He threw his arm over the floor, fingers digging in as he crawled free.

Then they were out of the hole. But he could not relax.

He lifted her and rushed out of the room, then the corridor, until the west wing was behind them. Only then did he sink down, Virtue cradled in his arms.

Anger filled him. He wanted to shake her and demand to know what she was thinking. Was she mad?

Did she not understand how dangerous it could have been?

How dare she traipse over what mattered to him?

Instead, his gloved fingers stiffly stroked through her hair, tangled by a burgundy ribbon.

She wore his gift!

Virtue's senses were returning. She groaned, her pallor chalky.

She put her hand to her lips, then she really saw him. Fright widened her eyes.

'I was searching for Imogen,' she gabbled. 'I saw . . . someone was there! I was falling and —'

'Hush. I feared you had perished. Never mind what led you there. Are you in pain?'

Concern smothered his anger. Nothing mattered so long as her eyes did not shut again.

She shifted, leaning away from him.

'I do not think — ah!'

'Where?'

'My knee. It must have been when I hit the floor.'

August's training in the Army had not

been forgotten. Just as if he was with a fellow male soldier he lifted her dress to the point just below her thigh.

With his more sensitive hand he probed the swollen, reddened knee.

'Not broken,' he murmured. 'Hopefully it's merely bruised.'

Her small gasp of surprise was what roused him from his examination.

He almost groaned. This was no man but a woman — his governess — whose good name and safety was under his charge.

But now was not the time and, besides, this was not someone deserving of his discretion. She was a spy.

Her beauty could not negate this truth.

He removed his hand.

'Forgive me, I was too hasty. I believed you damaged beyond repair.'

'You make me sound like a doll,' Virtue grumbled.

Somehow, he preferred this frustration to the dizzy, limpid creature he had pulled from the wreckage.

Propriety demanded he detangle

himself and summon a woman to tend to her.

His grip on her waist tightened.

'I must see to your injury. Once you are in bed I can —'

'No.'

His eyebrow lifted.

'You wish to continue to be in pain?'

'Of course not! Only, it would be improper for you to go into my room with me.

'Take me anywhere but there.'

A Soothing Salve

August picked Virtue up and strode down the stairs. He carried her to the library and laid her across the sofa.

The windows rattled from the thrusting of the wind.

'Wait here.'

He went to his study, where he kept an array of salves, and returned to her side.

He paused at the door, unnoticed by Virtue who was finally allowing the weariness of her trial to show as she leaned against the armrest, eyes half-lidded, face turned to the fire.

There was still time for him to summon a maid. Instead, he entered, his footsteps louder than they needed to be.

She started and tried to sit up, quick to conceal any weakness.

'Lie still, you'll only make it worse. This will dull the ache. It is St John's Wort, with parsley to help the bruise fade faster.'

'How do you know this?'

August unscrewed the small pot, revealing a pale coloured paste.

'When I was in the Army there were times our supplies were cut off. We had to rely on what we could find.

'Plenty of wounds that might have festered were cured thanks to the helping hand of the land.'

'You were a soldier?'

Virtue seemed about to say more but paused. She watched, amazed, as he tugged off his gloves.

The scars could not be ignored. They were vivid and violent and she stared at them fixedly, as though needing to prove to him they did not frighten her.

August could feel her eyes upon him. Miss Browne was good at hiding her disgust. She ought to be on the stage.

His fingers dipped into the pot, rubbing the paste together to warm it up.

This was not what he'd planned. He had meant to give the salve to her and leave.

It had been a long time since he had shown his hands and now he did it deliberately. Revealing his own secrets might make her admit a few of hers.

At least, with them both playing at pretend, he knew she would have to accept the state of his hands.

He cupped the tender flesh of her knee. Her gasp was cut short as her teeth sank into her lip.

'I was wounded by shrapnel from a musket backfire at Waterloo,' he told her, rubbing in small circles to spread the salve.

'What are you doing?' She was so quiet he had to strain to hear.

'I thought it quicker to do it myself. You need only ask me to stop.'

Her mouth opened, ready to force out the words. Instead, she looked away, the colour of poppies blooming on her cheeks.

A muscle in her leg twitched against his touch as she made herself be still.

He remained kneeling beside her, next to the sofa, not brazen enough to put her feet upon his lap.

This woman was his enemy yet he

could not deny his interest. He was attracted to the lie she had spun about herself: the headstrong governess he admired.

'I feared you were dead,' he murmured, voice rasping. 'Then I saw you there, still and pale. My heart stopped.'

'I'm sorry for causing you concern.'

'Are you?' he flashed. 'You did this to me constantly when we were younger.

'You affect me more with each passing day. No matter what I try to do, it is you who consumes my thoughts.'

The words flowed from his lips. Not all of this was deception. Somehow it was the truth.

Deception

Virtue stared down at her skirt. She could not bear to see what was happening.

Her other senses were honed in on August's ministrations. He must surely feel her trembling. Every thought and nerve seemed to centre on her knee.

Gone was the pain. There was only the coolness from the salve overlapped by the heat of his touch.

She felt a slight drag from where his scars caught her flesh, but it was gentle. Any source of discomfort came from herself.

There was no reason for feeling this way. He was merely tending to her injury.

She dared not speak, caught between wanting to keep him there and telling him to stop. Desire wanted the former, propriety demanded the latter.

Suddenly he was finished and rising. Her fingers curled tight to resist pulling him back. At least, with him out of reach, she found herself able to breathe again.

'I am much better, thank you,' she said, skirt thrown back over her legs. 'Goodnight. I will retire for now.'

As she tried to stand he firmly pushed her down, his hands once more gloved.

'It will take time for the salve to do its work. Do not undo what I have done.'

The door opened and Imogen stood there in her nightdress, hair loose and curling.

As she saw Virtue the cloudy gauze of sleepiness tore apart with her grin.

'Papa found you!'

Virtue forced a small smile.

'Yes, indeed he did. Are you heading for bed?'

The girl nodded enthusiastically.

'After my story.'

Virtue worried at her sleeves, horrified with herself. Had Imogen arrived any earlier she would have witnessed her governess and father in a compromising situation!

'Of course. I'll leave you two alone.'

August's hands did not leave her

shoulders.

'You do not mind sharing me with Miss Browne, do you, my dear?'

'No.' Imogen sat at the end of the sofa, beside Virtue's feet. 'Miss Browne, why are you lying down?'

'She has fallen and hurt her leg,' August answered for Virtue. 'So you will need to be good for her.'

'Yes, Papa.'

Imogen held out her book, demanding her story be read.

August settled himself in the chair opposite, his back to the fire and shadows dancing upon his face.

The story was of Old Shukka. Everyone along the coast knew of the beast.

The words flowed from him like gentle song. His listeners were there, running with the monstrous black dog through frosted woodland brittle as sugar upon glass.

Imogen's head drooped, but she forced herself up and staggered over to her father, squeezing in next to him. His hand rested upon her head.

Virtue watched them. At times she had been afraid of this man. Had been angered and upset. Now he showed another side to him.

Her own eyes were fluttering and her hand pillowed her cheek. The shadows of the room grew larger until even the lick of the flames became consumed.

★ ★ ★

Having returned from carrying Imogen to bed August stealthily re-entered the library, The fire had banked itself in the grate, its embers softening and brightening as though breathing.

Virtue still lay upon the sofa. Her hair had come free, spilling over the side to brush the floor. She had her head slightly tilted and her expression was lax and soft, lips parted. He saw the gleam of her teeth.

August stood watching her. Unsettled, he shook off the spell of her softened beauty.

He kneeled, catching up her hair and

the escaping ribbon.

Virtue stirred. The grey of her eyes swirled hazily.

'I am glad you enjoyed the gift,' he told her.

She blinked uncomprehendingly and he marvelled. So sweet did she look that he could believe there was no deception.

Instead of replying her face drew closer. Common sense cried for him to pull away but he remained still.

Virtue pressed her mouth to his. She tasted of lemon cakes, the same as Cook often made. That was what roused him, making him pause and break free to stare into her flushed, panting face.

They should not have done that.

'You cannot sleep here.'

Just as he had done with Imogen he lifted the governess into his arms.

He started briskly for her room, jostling her in his rush.

He thought she might protest yet not once did she speak.

Instead she watched him.

His heart quickened. The memory of the kiss thrummed over his lips.

But August would not take advantage of his friend. Even if she blindly followed Jeb's orders he would not have a part in ruining her.

What power did Jeb possess, to keep her in such thrall and risk her reputation?

August had encountered the type of woman Strawhouse kept in his orbit. Most were hardened by the hand Fate had dealt them.

Virtue did not seem like these women. Not yet.

He hefted her slightly to grasp the door handle. In response she pressed her face into the hollow of his throat.

He held her for a long moment, not wanting to release her comforting warmth. He must, though.

He had said what he needed only to lull her into lowering her guard. Anything further would be cruel.

Carefully, he laid her upon her bed. No longer did he feel her gaze upon him.

She had fallen back to sleep.

Unable to resist, he pressed a kiss to her forehead before departing.

What Happened?

Virtue stirred at the shriek of gulls. She tried to recall what happened last night but it merged with the blackness of her dreams.

There had been a storm. She remembered that most clearly.

She sat up and flinched at her sore leg. More memories returned. She had fallen through the floor in the west wing!

Another had been there, a stranger whose features were clouded. Then Lord Winterton had rescued her.

Virtue prodded at her leg. Her knee was puffy and a purplish red yet she only felt tenderness rather than constant pain.

Embarrassment coated her cheeks as she recalled August's tender ministrations and the sweet-smelling salve.

Why could she not forget that moment? Virtue would never be able to look at him again without knowing how close she had come to making a serious error in judgement.

Now roused, she braved the cold floor. Crumpled on the dressing-table were her gloves, tattered and grimy with dirt. They were beyond repair.

She went rooting through a drawer for her spare pair and something rolled out, clattering against the wood.

It was the ring August had given her that night at the inn. The fiery jewel in the centre was made of amber.

'The strength of a tiger.'

Perhaps what the Chinese believed was mere superstition but, after the night she had had, she could do with a good-luck charm.

Virtue put on the ring. It fitted tightly and would be hard to remove.

That might be misconstrued should August see her wearing this, she realised, and pulled on her fresh pair of gloves, covering the ring.

She felt better and almost stronger at the thought of her own secret to clasp tight.

In the schoolroom Virtue began lessons for the day. She paced, reading aloud from a book, while Imogen copied down the words.

Even with a slight limp, moving about helped her forget her discomfort both in flesh and mind.

Sunlight beamed into the room; the windows were thrown open to let in a brisk, healthy sea air.

The cry of gulls kept making Imogen stop and look. Virtue herself found it difficult to concentrate.

'Does your father mind you walking out?'

The girl seemed ready to lie but reconsidered.

'I do not know, Miss Browne.'

'Do you mean you never leave this house, Imogen?' she asked in disbelief. 'Have you ever been to the village?'

'I'm allowed to walk the gardens and ride my horse, so long as Papa can see me from the windows.

'I have all the company I need here,' she went on with vehemence.

'A woman will turn to parchment if she remains indoors too long.' Virtue helped her to put away her things.

'I will ask Lord Winterton to allow you to go to the beach.'

'But Papa . . . !'

'Do not look so stricken. I can quite easily persuade him to my way of thinking.'

'Can you, then?' a voice called teasingly. 'Am I truly wrapped around your finger?'

Virtue flushed in embarrassment. Lord Winterton was leaning against the doorway, idly tapping his boot with his riding crop.

He stared at Virtue, mischief in his eyes, while his daughter looked on with trembling admiration.

'Your daughter would benefit greatly from going outside,' she told him, ignoring his comment.

'Certainly,' he said, striding inside. 'The snowdrops have just begun to bloom.'

She searched his face for an answer as to what had transpired last night. There must be some way to tell.

His gaze fell to examine her lips rather than her eyes. Virtue stilled as that strange stirring sensation returned.

She forced herself to focus.

'While your grounds are most beautiful, sir, I was thinking of somewhere a little further.

'The beach, perhaps. As children we discovered all sorts of species in the rockpools, did we not?'

A hard edge entered his eye, soft green turning to glass. His lazy smile lost some of its geniality.

She fully expected him to argue, but he bowed his head.

'That is, of course, an excellent plan, but I do not think you should go alone. The dunes can be unstable.

'I will be happy to accompany you, Miss Browne.'

Dangerous Kisses

Lord Winterton sent orders to the kitchens for a picnic to be prepared. A basket was produced far quicker than Virtue expected.

Down to the beach they went until they found somewhere dry to lay their blanket. Imogen wanted to go explore but was forced to be still and eat first.

When she finally ran off to play Virtue was left with her father.

Although August had urged Imogen to eat he himself took nothing.

Virtue poured out a glass of ginger beer, its droplets splashing from a sudden gust. The spicy drink warmed her body, fizzing on her tongue.

'I do not remember much of yesterday,' she began, no longer able to delay. 'One moment I was falling and then I awoke in my bed as if it was a dream. What happened?'

'You were somewhere you shouldn't have been and the floor gave way. I tended to your injury.'

The roughness in his voice softened.

'Are you still in pain?'

Virtue studied him. He was concealing something but she sensed it was nothing as extreme as what she feared.

She smiled at August as he finally drank something.

'I am sorry for trespassing but I believed Imogen was there.'

'I am certain I locked the door.'

'It was open when I saw it, and I was not alone.'

Virtue noticed the tightening of his jaw.

'On the other side of the room, before I fell, I saw a woman. I cannot recall her entirely. I — I believe her hair was black.'

'Impossible!' he hissed.

Shakily he snatched a scone, scraping jam across the surface.

'You must have seen one of the family portraits. The storm tricked your imagination.'

Virtue hesitated, about to ask if the painting had been of Chastity, when he continued.

'Though there is a ghost in the manor.'

'A ghost?'

'Yes. The maids have seen her as well.' He bit into the scone. 'It is the spirit of a sailor's sweetheart, some girl who drowned while holding a lantern to guide the smugglers' ships.

'It may be best to think of her as a warning.'

'To smugglers?'

'And to those who help them.'

Virtue frowned and selected a sandwich stuffed with cold slices of beef.

She ate it in one go, chewing roughly.

'I should have thought the manor would have more ghosts.'

'Because you still believe the rumours?' he countered.

He smiled as she took a cheese sandwich then a strawberry tart, ravenously eating them one after the other.

'You've hardly given me reason to think otherwise,' she retorted.

August took another careful bite of his scone. He did not offer a response, perhaps enjoying the mystery.

Virtue picked another tart. She focused on the crumbling, crimped edging of the pastry rather than on August.

Her skin reddened under his gaze as it went from her cheek to her throat. It was as if he knew a secret, one to which she was not privy.

'You truly do not recall last night?'

'I must have hit my head when I fell.'

'You blame your actions on a head injury, then,' he pressed.

'My actions?'

He leaned in close, brushing aside a crumb at the corner of her mouth.

'You were daring enough to kiss me.'

'No! I —'

Warmth sank into the depths of her body as she finally remembered. The kiss came back as if she experienced it all over again.

'Do you regret it?' he asked.

Her hand slipped and her grey glove slid against a blackberry tart. She fussed with the material, trying to wipe off the stain.

'I do not regret it,' she admitted reluctantly, for she saw how his smile grew. 'But it should not have happened.'

'Why not?'

His frostiness had melted. Here was the man who had won her at the inn.

She had no idea what his true thoughts were about the kiss, whether he was pleased or merely enjoyed teasing her.

Lords might desire their governesses yet they never married them. She must be careful. She was only an amusement.

'Our ranks, sir. Kisses, soft as they are, are dangerous.'

August reached for her hand and she made to lean back.

'Hiding yourself away?' he challenged. 'I know what true horror looks like, remember. Don't tell me you cannot bear your own hands.'

He pinched one of the buttons and slid it through its hole. Then he pulled off the glove and scraped sand against the dark, blotchy stains to remove them.

Self-consciously, Virtue placed her other hand behind her. The one bearing the ring.

'They are a servant's hands. It is not what you are used to with your ladies from the ton.'

He laughed.

'I prefer a woman who knows work.'

Her wrist was red and chafed with an ink stain that had gone beneath the skin.

He stroked her knuckles. The swipe of his glove was cool and she felt every ridge in the stitching.

'You have broken your thumb in the past,' he mused, seeing the joint had not set in its proper place. 'Do you enjoy a good fight?'

That drew a laugh from her.

'During my travels there was a man who would not withdraw his attentions even when I begged him to stop. So I spoke in a more direct manner.

'And learned that day not to tuck my thumb into my fist!'

August ducked his head and kissed the slightly bent thumb. She inhaled sharply.

'I hope you knocked a few of his teeth loose as a reminder not to pester beautiful women. Though I cannot truly blame him.'

'I can!' she argued, unimpressed. 'If a man cannot understand the concept of not being wanted then he is too stupid to be allowed out of his house.'

'Does that include me? I have not set out to ruin you, Virtue,' he added when she was silent.

Her heart pounded. She wanted to give in to his kisses but to do so would be to surrender.

He must be playing with her. If he wanted anything it would be to make use of her and then abandon her.

At the thought of her old friend being like any other man Virtue became irritated. When his lips brushed her knuckles, she pictured Jeb gambling on her.

She snatched back her hand and pulled on her glove.

'That's enough,' she commanded. 'We are not two children at play any more. There are consequences.'

She had to retreat. Something deep within bristled.

Some sensation that she was being tricked, like a rabbit getting closer to a snare without realising.

She strode across the sands to join Imogen.

On the Beach

The sea was dark in the distance; high tide was due soon. Great bellyfuls of waves lapped over one another and the dampened sand Virtue and Imogen walked upon bore ripples scratched by the sea.

A crab, caught by the fury of the waves, lay upon its back amongst the stones, its shell cracked and legs crooked.

August did not join them. As Virtue glanced over her shoulder at him a glint of sunlight caught upon something he carried — a spyglass. She was not close enough to tell but sensed he was watching only her. She peered down at Imogen, pointedly ignoring him. 'Careful,' she teased. 'We wouldn't want the sea to nip you!'

Virtue recalled a game she, Jeb and August used to play. She inched towards the sea, stones clicking beneath her.

Gripping her skirts and raising them she revealed the ankle of her boot. And that is all August will ever see, she thought to herself wickedly. 'We will tempt the waves then race away from them!'

They edged closer, tense, ready to take flight. Water rushed over the stones, lunging over them.

Governess and student staggered back, their hands clasped, laughing and taunting as the wind-whipped sea spray grazed their cheeks.

Again they approached the waves, waiting until the last moment. Two waves came together, overlapping.

While one reached lazily for them the other surged forward, far too quick.

Virtue gripped the girl and swung her as high as she could. Seawater rushed over Virtue's boots and tangled with her skirts, crawling up her calves to sucker wool and linen to them.

The shock of the sudden cold made her shriek giddily while Imogen squealed.

Imogen's hair streamed over her face as she was set down, causing her to squint as she looked out to sea.

She clutched her skirt, one shoe sunken

in the wet sand. The wind tugged, whipping her lacy, pastel frills.

Virtue stooped to collect a shell spread out like a moth, the clasp as tiny as an eyelash.

Her head jerked as she heard Imogen call out excitedly.

'A ship!'

There was indeed one, so far off in the distance they could only see its fluttering sail.

The girl jumped and waved her hands as if the sailors might see her and wave back.

August approached, tucking the spyglass into his coat.

'It looks like you have lost your flirtation with the sea,' he remarked.

'Papa, can we do this again?' the child demanded.

'Did you enjoy yourself?'

At her vigorous nods, he smiled.

'Very well, if Miss Browne agrees, but we cannot be at play for ever. A storm is due.'

'The sky is quite clear, sir,' Virtue

145

argued. 'It will be fine weather, at least for tonight.'

'Always quick to discredit me in front of my daughter, are you not?' August teased lightly. 'Then let us say we will return because I wish it.

'Here, Imogen, run ahead. I will assist Miss Browne.'

The governess shook her head.

'I can walk, thank you.'

'You are soaked! And I suspect your leg still bothers you.'

'The wind will soon dry out my shoes.'

He did not argue. Instead, he wrapped his arms around her waist and heaved her into an embrace.

She sucked in her yelp of surprise so as not to give him the satisfaction.

Rather than relenting and looping her arms around his neck she crossed them pettishly. This served as a poor buffer.

'You are enjoying this,' she grumbled.

He grinned at her as a mischievous boy would. Her teeth ground together.

'Have you forgiven me?' he asked, voice soft and slightly uncertain.

'There are two sides of you, it seems,' she told him. 'Whom do you think I prefer — the one intent on tripping me up or the man who treats me as he would any his equal?'

That checked him. She saw his eyes widen but he hid his expression before she could work out what it was.

'Let us resume what was planned,' August said, evading the question. 'Come to my study once everyone is abed. I plan to sketch every facet of you.'

Laying a Trap

August stood at his study window. The night sky held no moon, its stars were dull.

He stared across the dark waters where he knew the *Reckless Mermaid* was anchored.

His pistols lay upon the desk. If Jeb dared trespass again it would lead to someone's death. For Chastity's memory and Imogen's sake he could not be caught off guard.

Capturing the smuggler before he revealed the truth meant he must quicken his pursuit of Miss Browne. August did not dare consider her feelings when his family remained in peril.

He wished there were some other avenue of attack.

A gentle rap roused him from his thoughts. August hid the weapons.

'Enter,' he commanded as though he had control over the situation.

How desperately he wished he had.

Virtue stood in the doorway, her shawl clasped tight. He noticed how the lace-like pattern was stretched over her hunched shoulders. She was as nervous as he was.

She glanced around, taking in the study, giving herself the chance to plan her strategy.

Little did she know of his trap.

There was a letter upon his table which contained details of the movement of confiscated brandy found submerged in a river. It had had a feather lure to mark the spot — a ruse known to smugglers as sowing the crops.

Virtue would see the letter and tell Jeb. August and his men would then ambush him when he came to reclaim the goods.

He must be patient. This time she would not fly from him.

'To be honest,' August began, 'I did not expect to see you, no matter your promise. This was not a usual request.'

'I never break a vow,' she replied, her composure recovered.

There must be resistance between

them. They might be strangers now, but some of the girl he had known must remain.

It had always been an argument which propelled Virtue into getting things done.

'Must I remind you it is my daughter you are educating and not me? It is arrogant to assume you can teach me anything.'

'This is for your daughter's benefit. She will suffer if you continue to shut yourself away. I am certain there is plenty you could teach me.'

Warmth settled around August's throat. He had to look out of the window.

This governess desired to learn much about her employer, he reflected.

'Why are you so invested in this?' he demanded. 'If I am to lay myself out to be scrutinised and judged then I expect something in return.'

She gave a weary but encouraging smile. But how could he trust this woman when all evidence told him not to?

'When a past misfortune is shared it

lessens the sting.'

He was silent and Virtue continued.

'I never got to say goodbye when we were children. Even though I had adventures across the sea there were many times I wanted to return.'

August indicated for her to sit and ready herself. He caught her looking at the letter, the flick of her eyes as she took in the words, yet her expression did not change.

She sat upon the window-sill, half-watching the sky for the rare glistening wink of a star.

'In China Father and I discovered cultures far more exotic than our own. I wish he had experienced the same wonder I felt.

'Instead he turned to drink.'

August dragged a chair to sit opposite her. With a sketchbook balanced upon his knee he flipped to one of the bare pages which used to taunt him.

He stiffly adjusted his rigid fingers until he could grip a pencil.

The first stroke had meant to be the

curve of her face but it wavered. Instead he made it end in a swirl to mimic loose strands of hair.

'I have not admitted this before,' she went on, 'but with Father no longer by my side I now know the truth. All my life he has been selfish.'

Out flowed the words. Of the nights Virtue had waited for her father's return, of the rages he fell into, of being unable to trust him to care for her.

'Which is why,' she finished, tiny breaths rushing out as she tried to hide her upset, 'I understand how a daughter feels when she is forced to suffer her father's miseries as well.'

The next pencil stroke was long and dark. As a boy August had only seen her father from a distance.

He now felt a deep anger towards this stranger.

Virtue turned aside.

He watched the gloved knuckle of her left hand rub her cheek. He became curious about the slight bump visible upon her ring finger.

'A model is not supposed to move about, is she?' Virtue apologised. 'You must be cursing me.'

'It would be impossible to capture your likeness if I did not include your need to be in constant motion.'

The pencil tapped against the paper.

'If speaking of troublesome things brings some relief . . .'

Virtue nodded, then stopped herself and resumed her earlier pose, still smiling as soft and patient as though he were one of her students.

So far August had managed to sketch half of her face and the delicate column of her throat. They were amateurish, rough strokes, barely keeping to the desired lengths.

Frustration prickled beneath the surface as he found himself unable to replicate what throbbed in his mind.

Rather than give into emotion, as he had done countless times before, he found himself telling Virtue what had led to his injuries.

He told her of the losses, how the men

he would meet one day and hear were dead the next. The choking endlessness of battle, smoke and fire and the salty bitter tang of sweat and blood.

It was a nightmare not even daylight could pierce.

'When the musket backfired I was badly wounded. I collapsed on the ground while the battle roared on around me.

'It was only afterwards, when the fighting finally stopped, that I was found and taken to a doctor. My father had given up on me.

'He did again when he saw I was a —'

August was unable to use the word his father had spoken, remembering the disgust on the man's face at the sight of his son's twisted hands.

'He should not have done so after everything you had been through,' she protested. 'You needed time to heal.'

'I have had nine years of it,' he remarked.

He hesitated as he put aside his pencil.

Like a boy needing his teacher's reassurance he almost offered to show her his work.

Roughly, he closed the sketchbook.

'I must not keep you, Miss Browne! You need your rest.'

'Might I see?'

'When it's finished,' he promised.

'Then I shall have to come again tomorrow so you can continue your work. Pleasant dreams, Lord Winterton.'

And they were pleasant, all of them featuring Virtue's tender smile and voice.

Beautiful

Time passed at Winterton Manor. Imogen was progressing in her studies and the west wing remained locked.

During the day Virtue's attentions focused upon Imogen. At night, though, they turned to the girl's father.

Tonight, the maid who had brought the tea left the room eyeing the pair suspiciously over her shoulder.

Virtue felt a ripple of embarrassment. She was only sitting for her employer, obeying her master's whims. There was nothing scandalous about this.

Yet when August sat near her, warm and smelling of woodsmoke, her body became plagued with the urge to touch and soothe.

Their nights together became as habitual as seeing the moon rise and the sun set, as if this had been and always would be part of their lives.

Imogen was only eight and would be under Virtue's tutelage for some time.

There would be no need to risk taking a step further into new, dangerous terrain.

At times she sensed an urgency to their meetings, as if August was nudging her into a corner. She had no idea what he wanted, even if she had suspicions.

He had not dared to kiss her but she felt his gaze as tangibly as any caress.

Governesses were not for marrying. If Lord Winterton was tempted to pursue her then she would have to run all the faster.

Reminding herself of what was at stake, Virtue pondered the awful things Jeb had told her about August.

She knew nothing of her employer's life outside of the manor, save for rumour.

'You've been kind to me,' Virtue told August once, 'yet others in the village would call you a brute. Cruel. Hedonistic.'

August paused, his thumb grey from smudging graphite.

'Does this come from Jeb Strawhouse?'

She shrugged.

'Not all of it. He said you were keen to hang criminals even for a minor crime. Is this true?'

His eyes flicked down, his pencil moving faster.

'Yes, I am known to be a strict judge.'

'Hanging is more than simply being strict. Could not these men have been rehabilitated?'

'You are one of those who dislike capital punishment? Examples must be made, especially towards smugglers,' he told her. 'I know why Jeb has the hangings on his mind. I sentenced one of his friends after he shot two customs officials.

'Do you not think those men's wives would prefer justice was served rather than seeing their killer go free?'

When they were not arguing Virtue listened to him talk about the myths he loved. She was lulled by the raspy, low tones of his voice.

'Those shadows beneath your eyes,' August observed one evening, 'are so dark they tempt me to try to wipe them off.'

Virtue swallowed, uncertain how to feel at the thought of him doing such a thing.

'I have difficulty sleeping. My dreams keep me awake.'

The nightmares — of a wolf in man's flesh, the tunnels where some fearsome beast roamed — spilled from her.

He listened, green eyes dark, lids half-shut.

'Perhaps I can allay your fears.'

He turned his sketchbook around for her to finally see.

'I have decided upon how I will make you immortal. We must return to below the dunes. You'll see for yourself nothing gruesome is lurking.'

Virtue leaned forward, eager to see if she might recognise the woman upon the paper. It distracted her from the fear of returning to those frigid passages.

She stared. It was an unsettling sensation, like watching a stranger and looking in a mirror. The face was the right size, eyes in the correct position. He had even captured the tiny curls of escaping hair.

The expression upon her face was not one she recognised. At least, it was one she had not realised others could see — pinched slightly in embarrassment yet smiling softly. Kind and, dare she say, alluring.

This was what August saw?

'I'm curious to see how you are able to transfer this to stone,' she murmured, knowing she would follow him no matter her hesitations. 'Thank you. It is . . .'

'Beautiful,' he answered for her.

★ ★ ★

That night, the cold deepened. Dogs nestled together before the kitchen fire and frost glistened on grass.

At sea the waves were black and still. A shudder of white floated across. The snows had arrived.

Virtue remembered how icy it had been within the tunnels the deeper they had gone. August planned to lure her to its darkest depths and only he knew the way back to daylight . . .

His shifting moods left her uncertain whether she should anticipate his anger, be lured by his sweet teasing or thrum with excitement from the mysteries he promised.

Had she been a girl she would have demanded an explanation. As a woman and governess she had learned to hold her tongue.

Perhaps this was why young women faced so many difficulties. It was frowned upon to be clear and direct; everything must be veiled with respectability or ignored entirely.

Honesty was refreshing. August had been daring enough to treat her as a friend.

He might prefer her straightforwardness. And if he did not then she must stir his gentler notions.

Folded in her luggage was the cape he had given her after their first encounter. She slipped it around herself.

On instinct, her face pressed against

the collar. It smelled faintly of him. She shut her eyes and willed her flush to leave.

Composed once more, Virtue hurried from her room and down the dark stairs.

From the window, she saw the bobbing of a lantern. Might the lighthouse-keeper be watching tonight?

If he was, no doubt he would believe another woman had been carried off to an awful fate.

A Cry in the Tunnel

The flame guttered in August's lantern. A figure hurried to meet him, glancing at the sleeping house as though afraid it would wake and catch her in the act.

As a boy, August had crept down the ivy and near broken his neck whenever he escaped to see Virtue and Jeb.

Now he was master here. There was no need to skulk about, yet he also felt the urge to be quiet.

As he took in what Virtue wore he smiled. He slowly swung the lantern, indicating for her to follow.

They made their way through the tunnels, Virtue's footsteps echoing behind his. She stared resolutely ahead.

Then they were in the cavern of statues, where the chair and block of stone awaited.

Without prompting she took her place and, from the folds of his cape, produced a book to occupy herself.

'You're not too cold?' August asked.

'No, sir. I only wonder at how I can stay still for so long.'

His gloved fingers made a final adjustment to the cape around her shoulders before he went to the stone.

Virtue bent her head to read and August picked up his chisel.

He soon felt the undercurrent of a dull ache yet agony did not come. This would be a test of mind, body and willpower.

Virtue sat as she had done when he watched her through the damask curtain. He saw her nervousness no matter how still she kept herself.

If she cringed or fretted he would stop. An unwilling model tainted the work.

As if sensing his thoughts she scowled at him and straightened herself.

August made the first cut, the vibration of the strike jarring through him.

He would not be able to capture her entirely before succumbing to his pains. It was impossible; why try?

But Virtue was willing to brave her fears. He must do the same.

August needed to find the softness of

her cheek and, somehow, transmute it to stone.

Stroke the feathers of her eyelashes, caress the dip where shoulder met throat to capture the flicker of her pulse . . .

He made another cut.

* * *

Virtue slowly turned the page of her book, hopefully revisiting where she had left off. But the story made no sense to her.

Her skin itched. A strand of hair tickled and her legs were aching. Somehow, without doing anything she was exhausted.

What could be heard, between the jarring snaps of the chisel, was the flutter of her breaths, the scraping rustle of the book and the distant drum of falling water.

Nerves taut, she tried to see what August was doing out of the corner of her eye. All she saw was an impression.

The weight of his attention on her

skin was maddening. She anticipated his physical touch then became frustrated when it did not come.

Virtue stilled, her breath caught in her throat. She had heard something from one of the other tunnels. A moan!

It came again just when she thought she might be mistaken.

August was fixated upon his sculpture and must not have heard, or else it happened so often it no longer perturbed him.

The sound returned as a weak, whining cry. Virtue's nails dug into the book's binding.

The lighthouse-keeper's wife returned to her thoughts with her tales of captive women scratching to be released, locked somewhere deep in the ground.

Might they have stayed missing because they were trapped in these statues?

August's chisel scraped against stone. Shards flew as the hammer hit its mark and the high-pitched note of metal rang out.

It could be mistaken almost for the scratch of some creature's claws.

'Have you tried working here recently?' she asked.

'On and off. Without a model there was no drive.'

Virtue listened carefully. The cries became harsher, less human. It was the wind!

Outside, as the weather worsened, gusts ricocheted within the passages and crevices, the sound becoming otherworldly.

The illusion had been spun by her mind's desire to trick her. Anything could be imagined if you wanted to believe.

August called for Virtue to relax. Hours must have passed yet throughout this it had felt as if she had been suspended in time.

The stone block had broken away into the outline of a woman. Her throat and the curve of her cheek were revealed along with a single strand of hair.

Of course August would not be finished after one session. Which meant she would have to go through this again.

She swallowed down the mix of emotions the prospect stirred.

When the session was finished they returned to the manor and Virtue entered her room.

Wearily, she untied the cape and shrugged it off, then she bent to light a candle.

The flame wavered, casting a dull, flickering eye upon her surroundings. The darkness leached away.

One shadow, which bore the shape of a sleeping woman did not disappear. Gold gleamed.

Someone had been in her room again! Had August commanded one of the maids to do this?

A stunning dress the tawny colours of dawn had been laid across her bed.

The collar was ringed with gauz and lace and peppered with pearls.

Pinned to the breast was a mask edged with feathers, the nose curved to resemble a beak.

A pair of elbow-length gloves were

folded on the pillow. The fingers curled around a letter.

You are invited to the winter celebrations. Leave behind your face and past, for tonight you will be another person entirely.

And, Virtue reflected, in such a situation anything could happen.

Courting a Spy

'You wanted me to stop hiding away, Miss Browne,' August retorted when she demanded why he had invited her.

He grimaced.

'Amazing how the gulls swarm around an unattached man! It seems I have more friends than I realised.

'At least it is for charity. Donations will be sent to the Foundling Hospital.'

Virtue was perplexed. Governesses did not belong amongst music and laughter and dancing. They were the true ghosts of a household.

She should be pleased for August. He might dance with a young lady of his rank and . . .

Something clenched within her chest as she accepted that, selfishly, part of her wanted to keep him and Imogen to herself.

If this was a challenge, she could not run.

The tawny dress had been moved to

170

hang over her door, her gaze drawn back to it constantly whenever she tried concentrating on other matters.

When she held the mask to her face another woman looked back from the mirror.

Instead of someone uneasy and out of place, a stranger smirked. Attractive and confident, anticipating what was to come.

A flurried knocking startled her.

'Come in, Imogen.'

The moment the child took in her dress her eyes widened.

'So I'm the only one who has to go to bed early! Not fair!'

'When I get the chance I'll hide you somewhere quiet.' Virtue held out her hands. 'I know nothing of dancing. Perhaps you can show me?'

Cheered, Imogen took her hands and the pair spun around the room, laughing.

* * *

The study door opened.

'Papa, may I ask something?' a timid voice called.

August stilled. The dog he petted grumbled in annoyance, nudging him with her snout.

He feared Virtue was missing again. She got herself in too many difficulties. One day she would not escape unscathed.

But Imogen was not wiping away tears from those blue eyes which reminded him so much of her mother.

There were times he had to stop himself calling her Chastity. Maddening that a child's face could thrust him into the past, bringing with it the guilt he constantly battled.

He could only hope he had done right by Chastity and her daughter.

'What is the matter?'

She pinched at her gloves, fraying the holes where her fingers emerged.

'Will you ask her at the party?'

'Ask who?' His smile ebbed.

'Miss Browne! It is what people do in books. Then you can marry in the new year.'

He felt as though he was speaking with a woman rather than a child.

'What makes you think there will be a marriage?'

'I — I have seen you.'

His mind raced to work out what she might have seen.

'The way you smile at her. I've heard you as well. You know Miss Browne!'

'Of course I know her, she is your governess.'

'But from when you were children. Tell me about it.'

'What is it you wish to know?' he asked.

'Tell me about when you were my age.'

His throat tightened.

'Well, Virtue was one of the village girls. We used to play together on the beaches — explore caves, run across the dunes.

'It was very pleasant to see her again.'

He did not dare say much. For it was not merely two children at play. To see her upon the beach had felt the same as watching the dawn appear.

Imogen nodded.

'I think, if I should ever marry, I would want them to be a friend.'

One day, would she detest August for all he had done to keep her safe?

She clasped her hands.

'Please do not send Miss Browne away like you have done the others! I like her and she is nice to me. I do not mind if she has to become my mother.'

He kneeled so they were eye to eye.

'I understand why you like her company. I am happy in her presence as well.'

He stroked the hair from her face.

'No matter what I decide,' he continued, 'your mother will never be replaced.

'Other women may love you and treat you as their daughter. It is all right to love them back, but they are not replacements.'

'Yes, Papa.'

'If I were to ask Miss Browne to be my wife . . .' sweat gleamed on the back of August's neck '. . . would you be upset? Do not say what will please me. I want to know what you truly want.'

She thought a while and he was forced

to stay still and try not to let his inner thoughts show on his face.

'I would not mind her marrying you, Papa, so long as she still taught me.'

He pressed a kiss to her forehead.

'Thank you. Do not tell Miss Browne about this conversation just yet. It will be our secret.'

The girl giggled, enjoying the subterfuge, and ran out.

August rocked back on his heels and covered his face. He had thought he was being subtle!

The wooing of Miss Browne might have begun as a way to gain her trust but it had turned into something else.

Although, to be precise, it was his daughter who spoke of marriage.

He had courted a spy in order to ensnare her but now found he was the one trapped.

No matter how much he tried to cast her as the seductress, the traitor, Virtue was still the girl he had fallen in love with all those years ago.

He had known all along that chasing

her held the promise of another ending than simply capturing Jeb.

It would not be as simple as proposing to the young woman. August would be happy to deal with the gossips over a lord marrying his governess.

The problem was she was loyal to his enemy.

A shudder began in his hand. Distantly he heard a ringing noise. Blurriness crept into his vision, paintings and curtains merging with one another.

August escaped his study and strode jerkily to the governess's room, not knowing what he did.

The door was half-open. His trembling hand lifted to rap. Just as his knuckles scraped the wood, he discerned a shimmering movement through the gap.

Virtue spun around, the dress he had chosen swirling with her. She was beautiful. He would need to ensure she was not overwhelmed by the hordes of men who would be certain to approach.

August banished such a vulgar, possessive thought. What came next was an image of them greeting the arrivals as lord and lady of the home, their arms entwined.

He must be stronger than this! At any moment, Jeb might remove her from the vicinity of the attack.

Virtue was worth more than a rogue like Strawhouse. If she would not have August, still he would free her from the smuggler's clutches.

Lady Romana

The grasses had shrunk back, their deadened colours coated in snow. Sand glistened with a touch of frost. Ice floes swept back and forth on the waves, breaking into shards with each thrust.

Where, before, not a soul dared brave the incline leading to Winterton Manor, carriages now heaved themselves nose to tail.

Imogen watched from between the banisters. She had dressed herself in her finest.

Her nose scrunched up.

'I thought they would be more special,' she told Virtue, 'like peacocks.'

'They strut as those creatures do!' Virtue took the girl's hand. 'Hurry now, before we are seen.'

They crept downstairs and entered the ballroom. The windows looked over the dunes, creating the trembly, flimsy sensation of dangling on the edge.

Imogen ducked underneath a curtain.

Virtue sneaked her a glass of watered down orgeat syrup and a small cake from a table laden with treats.

Guests rushed in much the same as water over a brook. One by one candles were extinguished, smoke writhing.

It would be easy to mistake someone for a shadow.

There were finely dressed deer, hares and swans. When a rare flickering light caught their masks feathers and sequins gleamed. Laughter came harsh like crows.

'Shh!' Virtue whispered as there was a rustle behind the curtain and another giggle. 'I will get in trouble if your father catches us.'

The girl kept peeping out, transfixed by the pretty masked creatures and twinkling decorations.

Virtue had been more interested in trying everything laid out on the banquet table. Her lips felt sticky from plum juice while her tongue fizzed with sugar.

She had refrained from drinking yet she still felt lightheaded.

'You seem lost, my dear,' someone said.

Virtue turned, her mask flush to her face as she forced a smile.

'Please do not worry. I'm unused to crowds. This is a marvellous party.'

The other woman's mask had been tied to her hair with ribbons and split apart into moth wings. The lace edging of her fan tickled her wide, red-painted lips.

Soft eyes with thick lashes narrowed.

'I think you've done enough now,' she whispered. 'Your friends will be waiting.'

'Excuse me?'

'Surely this is a jape concocted by the servants? You look very nice for a maid but you'd best hurry before the dress's real owner comes down for the party.'

'A servant would be more respectful than you,' Virtue said bluntly.

The woman stiffened. She was about to respond when another approached.

'My dear Lady Romana, I am pleased to see you.'

The man wore a simple black mask

yet Virtue knew his voice, his eyes.

She even recognised the way he held himself so his hands were half-hidden: one upon his chest, the other behind his back.

Lord Winterton's clothes resembled a soldier's uniform but the coat was dark rather than red, embroidered with a flower design. At his lapel was a deep red rose.

Virtue's throat tightened, recalling a Persian poem about a nightingale and a rose.

She looked to the moth, thinking he had spoken to her. However, August held his hand out to Virtue.

'Lady Romana?' the other woman echoed. 'I am not familiar with the name.'

'You would not be. Her family are close friends of mine new returned from China.'

'The poppy fields? Ah, new money.'

'My Lady would not sully herself with that barbarous trade.'

August clasped Virtue.

'Come, I demand a dance.'

Virtue glanced back, searching for Imogen. The child remained hidden, a pair of wide eyes peeking out.

Her grinning mouth told her to go.

August held Virtue close and she found herself relenting. She took his hand, her fingers entwining with his.

In that almost darkness it was as if they were the only two there.

'I am a lady now, am I?' she asked, lips close to his ear.

'Well, seeing as I cannot strip these lords and ladies of their titles, for tonight you have been elevated.'

'I still do not know why you invited me.'

'Because you are the only reason I am here,' he told her.

Virtue peered over his shoulder, only just noticing they were beside one of the many windows. The moon showed their reflections.

They seemed entirely different people, not a lord and his governess, but lovers.

It was too shadowy to perform the more open quadrilles, where dancers flitted about one another like birds, snatching compliments as they passed. This forced people closer, into intimacies they might not have dared in the full glare of light.

'Why invite these people?' she wondered. 'You are master here.'

'Master only of this lonely, insignificant house on a rock. Hardly the best of things to offer someone.'

Before she could respond women surrounded them. Leading them was the moth-masked woman.

Virtue's stomach lurched in annoyance.

'Do not be selfish, August,' the stranger said. 'We are all eager to meet Lady Romana.'

Random women gripped her hand and petted her cheek as though they were sisters. They pulled her into a swarm of pastel-shaded, feathered masks of pretty creatures. Gossip lapped in waves.

August followed but stayed distant. He leaned against a pillar, watching with amusement but ready to swoop if needed.

'You have not been in England long?' one lady enquired.

'No,' Virtue answered. 'I only returned due to home sickness.'

'Then you have not heard about the Heartgood family!'

Virtue was regaled with gossip of people she knew nothing of and did not care to: the old man had gambled his money away, the youngest daughter was shamefully involved in politics and the only son and heir had absconded to avoid his debtors.

'He took his sister's maid with him. Someone swears they witnessed their marriage in Scotland!

'He'll rue this. They might look as we do but servants are from a different plane.'

The moth was watching her.

'A maid has a simple country sweetness that is appealing,' she said over her fan. 'At least they are innocents led astray and easy enough to manage.

'It is when men dabble with governesses that they suffer.'

'What makes a governess so different
from a maid?' Virtue snapped.

'They are a conundrum. Not quite
a lady, not quite in the gutter. Bitter
women desperate to claw back respectability and steal another's roof to keep
over their head.

'They thrust themselves into society
when they are no longer welcome.'

A few of the other women made
sounds of agreement, recalling their own
sour-faced governesses.

'In my opinion it is admirable a young
woman uses her skills and knowledge to
support herself, rather than be a burden.

'I suspect someone's distaste for governesses stems from some fear that the
same 'poor fate', as they perceive it, will
befall them!' Virtue responded.

Red patches of annoyance began to
emerge from around the edges of the
women's masks.

Virtue was about to go on when a sudden sound jolted through her.

It came again and, embarrassed, she covered her mouth as another hiccup escaped.

Amusement rippled amongst the ladies at her discomfort.

The moth smiled sweetly at her.

'A touch nervous, my dear?'

August approached. He held out his hand to guide Virtue away.

'We will find some means of relieving you of your discomfort.

'I do not blame you. I've been less afraid of dealing with a nest of adders than mingling!'

Then the lord and his governess were out of sight, leaving the women alone and feeling vaguely slighted.

A Cure for Hiccups

August led Virtue through the ghostly vision of the other dancers. A curtain lifted and fell.

They had to rely on touch, a hand upon his arm, clasping the hidden muscle there, or the faint caress on her lower back as he guided her.

Virtue's mask wavered in her grip. She leaned over, taking in breaths, yet the vexing popping sound continued.

August returned with a glass filled with water.

'Here. Slowly, though.'

She rubbed at her red cheeks and streaming eyes, coughing.

'I've caused such a scene!'

'Nonsense. You did nothing wrong.'

'Not that they cared,' she reflected. 'I am not their sort.'

'Those ladies should be thankful. Your voice was taken momentarily so they would not have to suffer being bested by someone with more wit.'

Laughter erupted from her, jerking with her hiccups. It all seemed so ridiculous.

August grinned in response.

'That is what I like to see,' he rumbled.

'Must we go out there again?' Virtue pleaded. 'Can we not remain here and hope they leave?'

'We may. I am lord over all here.'

She supposed this was what he had been like as a young man, confident and thinking he may do what he liked. Not hidden away, shunning all humour and affection.

She mourned the loss of his innocence but preferred the man who stood before her.

'And do I come under this claim?' she challenged.

'Only if you wish to be.'

He leaned in and now nothing separated them save their own insecurities.

Quick to get away from that subject, she smiled.

'Thank you for giving me the dress. It

is beautiful.'

'Do you know what creature you are?' he asked.

She did know, yet evaded the question.

'You are not an animal at all. You seem to revel in being different from the rest of us.'

'But I lie in the breasts of all men and women. I am the flower of love.'

'Or rejection,' she countered, then realised she had revealed too much.

'Would you really reject me, Virtue?'

She shivered. They spoke each other's surnames so much that to hear him speak her Christian name made it sound so intimate.

'August,' she murmured low, her eyes hooded.

He cupped her chin between his thumb and finger. No longer could she hear the music or the gossiping.

The colour of his eyes kept changing in the shadows. She tried to work out what the shade reminded her of.

They were dark, dragging her beneath the surface as marsh weeds would cling to an unwary traveller.

He came closer and their lips brushed . . .

A final hiccup rattled through her. They broke apart and she covered her mouth. They both began to laugh at the absurdity of the moment.

As she stood, her eyes wet and face pink with joy, August dived down and crushed their mouths together.

Virtue had only been kissed once, a stolen kiss, and had been dazed on the occasion she dared to try it herself. She would not let this one slip away.

All common sense called her a fool. She would be tainted if he cast her aside.

Should she even consider surrendering?

When they broke apart again Virtue cupped his cheek.

'I want you.'

The kiss was softer this time, triumphant. She happily sank into his embrace.

She did not notice her mask slip from her hand, nor hear the sharp rattle of it hitting the ground.

The curtains were ripped back. Miss Moth stood there, mouth open in derision and glee.

'Goodness,' she said breathlessly as the pair quickly parted. 'I did not think hiccups were cured by that!'

Ashamed, Virtue rushed off and forced her way through the crowd. She had to find Imogen.

Another wave of guilt washed through her. She should be caring for her charge, not seducing the girl's father!

* * *

She discovered Imogen still hiding behind the curtain. The child's face was half-buried in the material, eyes flickering sluggishly.

Sugar smeared her mouth which she clumsily wiped off.

'It is time for bed for both of us,' Virtue coaxed.

She clasped her hand and led her to the door, ignoring the girl's faint, half-yawned protestations.

They were almost there when a man stepped before them. He wore the mask of a fox.

His thin lips were stretched into a smile, deepening the hollows of his eyes.

'A pleasure to meet you, my Lady.'

He took her hand, the one holding Imogen, forcing her to let go.

'Is this beautiful child yours?'

He was a Frenchman, Virtue realised as he kissed the back of her glove. That should not make her instantly mistrust him — the war had been nine years ago — yet something about him made her want to back away.

'She is my master's child.'

'Oh? I knew the family once. I did not hear the young lord was married.'

Imogen leaned against Virtue's hip, almost asleep.

'Yes, sir,' Virtue answered. 'To a Lady Chastity. Imogen is their child.'

The man's eyebrows shot up.

'Surely you jest. Chastity Winterton was his sister, there's no doubt about that.

192

'Did the young lady have her out of wedlock? Is he merely a guardian?'

Imogen could not hear this slander.

'Please stand aside, sir,' Virtue demanded. 'The child is tired.'

He did so with a bow but watched them leave, his eyes narrowed upon Imogen.

Virtue almost ran, half-carrying Imogen, to her room. She glanced back, afraid the Frenchman would follow.

The girl sleepily embraced her then crawled into bed. Virtue could only hope she was too sleepy to have heard what the stranger said.

There must be some mistake, Virtue repeated to herself as she entered her own room. Said it again and again until she fell asleep.

Had August been lying to her all this time?

Later that night a pistol shot jolted her awake.

Virtue's heart squeezed. Her first thought, as her fuddled senses crept back, was that it was a tiger! Another had tried breaching the camp.

Only then did she recognise her room in Winterton Manor.

She staggered from her bed and stumbled through the darkened corridors. The shot still rang in her ears.

Other guests emerged from their rooms, bleary and uncertain. One of the dogs paced, growling and sniffing the air. It knocked aside something on the ground which clattered at Virtue's feet.

Lord Winterton stood at his daughter's door with a pistol.

'What's going on?' Virtue demanded. 'Is Imogen safe?'

'Cease your questioning,' August said without even looking at her. 'There was an intruder and I've seen him off. That is all you need to know.'

'Let me check on my student!'

He would not move. Finally, their eyes met. His teeth were gritted as if she was the one at fault.

'She does not need you,' he told her. 'You are not her mother.'

Virtue would not be dissuaded. People eyed them, the worst-minded of them clearly believing it to be a lover's quarrel.

'I refuse to live here a moment longer,' she seethed, 'without knowing what goes on beneath this roof!'

'Then perhaps you should go.'

The fury on his face stilled and quickly fled.

'Virtue —'

She stiffly called for the guests to return to their beds, there would be no more excitement tonight.

Sighing, August opened Imogen's bedroom door and entered, closing it behind him.

As Virtue was leaving she glanced down. There, on the floor, was the Frenchman's fox mask.

Chastity's Child

Virtue waited for dawn to creep between her curtains before she emerged.

She had not packed her bags and absconded in the night after August's cruel rejection, though that had been her first urge, especially after what had transpired at the party.

This was her home as well. And Imogen deserved so much more. To go beyond these gardens that steadily eroded; to know more than a crumbling home and a father who showered her with love then vanished as a ghost did.

The truth of her mother must be known.

Though it might be Virtue's own selfish desire to sate her curiosity, she hoped some good might come of this.

Imogen's door was barred to her, a dog guarding it. August had pulled up his fortifications.

It seemed the closer they became, the further they ran from one another.

When she passed the remaining guests they looked upon her with disdain, a disgrace no doubt they hoped their daughters would not become.

From the window she saw Mr Charles make his way past the gardens and towards the beach.

He had tried to speak to her about Chastity as if to warn her.

Virtue hurried after him, barely remembering to put on her warmest cloak on. The wind blew fiercely.

'Please, slow down a moment! I must ask something of you.'

'You've angered the master again,' Mr Charles remarked, eyes narrowed. 'He doesn't like people interfering.'

'I'm afraid it is my way. I must understand what has taken place in this house — what grips it and keeps it locked in this almost-frozen state.'

'Grief and guilt are mighty strong things,' he replied. 'I'll tell you, if you follow me.'

They walked across the beach. Sand fell away beneath their boots, some pockets deeper than others. Virtue clutched her skirt as she tried to keep her balance.

Past the shingle she saw something abandoned on the sands. Dark red seaweed stretched out, wet and frayed.

'Chastity was the twin of your Lord Winterton,' Mr Charles told her. 'Wild and reckless even with her . . . complications.

'Her father let her do as she pleased so long as no-one found out.'

'I never knew of a sister! Surely they didn't hide her away?'

Mr Charles offered no answer but continued his story.

'On the day she was meant to be married off she revealed she was pregnant with another man's child.

'Not so wild then — instead, desperate and begging for mercy. The old lord threw her out.'

'Who was the father?' she gasped.

The cold was so sharp it pinched the breath from her; her throat was sore and scraped.

'A poor local fisherman. August

argued for his sister's sake but his father wouldn't relent. So he hid her in the tunnels.

'Something must have happened. An argument, perhaps. August staggered into the house soaked in blood and clutching the child.'

Relief flooded through Virtue. Imogen was his niece! It was a good deed he had done in taking her on.

Yet, her thoughts whispered as they crunched across the pebbles, it did not absolve him completely. What had befallen Chastity?

'How did she die?'

Virtue suspected the old man was taking her somewhere as explanation. To the place the woman had died, or even her hidden, shameful grave.

A dark shape was anchored in the waters, swaying gently. So black it seemed a shard of night arrived early.

Waves slowly reared then tumbled down, spray glistening with the light of the greying day. More of the stringy red seaweed clung to the backs of the waves.

Virtue stopped following Mr Charles.

He was taking her to the ship Imogen had spotted that day on the beach.

All common sense warned her to return to Lord Winterton.

Behind her was the rise of the dunes. All around were flat sands and an endless stretch of sea.

Another figure walked towards them with frayed nets hanging from his shoulder.

Virtue ran. Harold Charles swore, calling her to come back like a dog to heel.

The man with the nets raced to catch her.

Jeb wrapped his arm around Virtue and she shrieked, banging her fists against his head.

The gardener caught up and she was no match. Jeb's net was thrown over her, thrusting her to the ground. Rough grains of sand cushioned her aching cheek.

They scooped her up and carried her away.

Capture and Escape

Tangled like a captured mermaid, in Jeb's mocking words, Virtue was taken to the ship.

They heaved her up the gangplank, unsteadily making their way across the deck which dipped and rose.

A cabin door banged open, then the sky was gone and she was within the belly of the ship.

She had been taken to the captain's quarters. Jeb thrust her into a chair and went to the desk.

He set his hands upon the salt-engrained wood, idly stroking the bronze statuette of a leviathan.

When he met Virtue's eyes he smiled almost fondly.

'My apologies for the rough journey,' he remarked, mimicking a gentleman even with his rough accent. 'Winterton left me with few choices.'

Virtue pried the brine-soaked net from her face and tried to kick her legs free.

She knew she was crying, half from the seawater that had got into her eyes and half from panic.

Desperately she thought of how to calm him. A memory flashed of a letter on Lord Winterton's desk about some evidence being moved.

Might he release her if she gave him this information in exchange?

But her mouth remained closed. She would not betray August.

'This is all mine, Virtue,' Jeb continued. 'See how I've risen, without need of titles or fawning to my betters. My men call me the Lord of the Sea.'

'All of it bought from stolen things and men's blood,' Virtue spat. 'It is cursed.'

'How else do men like me escape the gutter?'

He made no move to approach yet she feared he might grab her if she did not keep him in her sights.

'I know you despise me for refusing to bend to your will, but do you think you can bargain with August?

'I assure you, it will not work. I am

merely his governess. You would do better to release me.'

He turned aside and, of all things, laughed.

Virtue did not respond. She craned her neck to look around, quickly taking in her surroundings.

The door was open yet she saw the shoulder of a guard as he shifted. A pistol was on the table but Jeb was closer to it than she was.

There was a bed, unmade, and a bottle lay on the pillows. A collection of spyglasses sat on a shelf, rolling back and forth from the swaying of the ship.

She looked to him again as he turned back to her.

'My dear, those lies must taste bitter on your tongue. My associate, Mr Leroux, saw how in thrall August was to you during the dance. How you clung to him.

'And I shall use that to get what I want.'

'Which is?'

'My daughter.'

Imogen? She gasped.

'No!'

'Why offer them loyalty? She is not your child. She is not even Winterton's. She belongs with her true father.

'Had he not hidden her for so long I would have claimed her sooner. A step-child would only get in the way of your ambition. We can help one another.'

'How can you be Imogen's father?'

'Not everything is about you,' Jeb said spitefully. 'I'm not a lovelorn fool like August was, clinging to the hope you would return.

'Chastity lit the way for the ships and found hideaways for my goods. She thought it all a grand adventure, the empty-headed fool!'

'Do not mock the dead.'

'Don't you agree a daughter should be with her father? I am all the girl has left. Were it not for August's jealous meddling then she would be in my possession.

'I thought spreading a few rumours would get the villagers to chase him off.'

'Why did Chastity run from you?'

He scowled, lips drawing back to

show tobacco-stained teeth. His knuckles rubbed across the broken bent of his nose.

'It was a mere argument. She overreacted and ran her mouth to her family. Much good it did her.'

Virtue should not be arguing with him. He was dangerous.

If she pretended to go along with his plans she could escape and warn August.

Jeb sneered as if he knew exactly what she was thinking.

'Why should I explain myself to you? I'll not offer you inducements. There's no need to waste my money. Your life is worth much more.'

Virtue's throat knotted. She clasped her hands together as he crept closer.

'You will return to the house,' he ordered. 'No tears will be shed. Winterton won't know what has taken place.

'When you next see my daughter you'll take the girl through the tunnels. Then we'll be off to France, never to return.

'You may join us. It would make her

calmer and be easier to avoid questions if others think you her mother.'

He saw her disgust and smiled thinly.

'My men will take you back and hide themselves upon the grounds, so remember to hold your tongue.'

He left with his pistol, the door shutting. She heard the harsh scrape of a lock.

Virtue kicked off the last of the net. She paced, searching for some means of escape.

A breeze scrabbled in from the tiniest of openings. She heaved the window open the rest of the way and peered outside.

The waters were so dark not even the lights coming from the ship were reflected. She searched for the shoreline, praying they hadn't hauled anchor and started to drift.

Jeb needed her reinstalled at Winterton Manor so hopefully it meant they were close enough to land.

What she planned was madness, yet it was her only means of freedom.

She removed her dress. All she kept on was her chemise.

She braced her foot on the window's edge, then jumped.

A Deadly Gamble

A shadowy figure dived and there was a splash, alerting one of the sailors on deck. When no cry for help came he continued his work, blaming the noise on a seal.

Virtue broke the surface, spitting seawater. Something brushed her thigh and she carefully angled herself before kicking out. If the seaweed caught her she would be ensnared.

There were shouts overhead; Jeb had returned to his cabin. She gritted her teeth, swallowing her panic.

Another splash came, the sound of a rowboat being winched down. A dog barked as lanterns were raised.

Virtue carefully turned on her back. The murky sky, hazy with sparse smatterings of emerging daylight, stared down at her as she paddled with her feet. Waves rocked her from side to side.

It felt as if she would be like this for ever but finally shingle scraped her back.

Her toes dug into sand as she forced herself to stand, only to cry out as she stumbled over a patch of prickly salt-wort.

Red glistened on the imprint of her next step.

Virtue would not look over her shoulder. She knew, if she did, she would see the rowboat cleave through the sands, a single man and his huge dog leaping out to give chase.

She heaved herself up the slight incline but the softer sands gave way, tripping and winding her.

She crawled instead until she reached the top and slid down.

Bushes and grasses trembled at the shaking of the winds. She crouched, knowing she should not stop but needing to breathe. Her hand covered her mouth.

The dog emerged first. He stood on the slight hill, fur ruffled as if made of smoke.

Shuck bent his head, his nose flaring.

Virtue crept backwards. The sharp

scratch of brambles caught her shoulder.

The dog drew closer, snuffling the ground as he followed her scent. She put her thumb and finger together and whistled.

Shuck jerked, his paws pounding as he raced towards the sound.

Virtue held herself still until, at the very last moment, she dived to the side just as the dog leaped, his teeth flashing as they gnashed together.

The poor creature tumbled into the bramble patch and was soon caught up.

He bit and kicked but could not get himself free.

She felt miserable at the dog's suffering. His only mistake was loyalty to his master.

She hurried away, knowing Jeb would be drawn to the noises.

He was and, soon enough, he approached the whining dog. Virtue could hear him as she ran across the dunes.

A single light blazed in Winterton Manor. As Virtue ran it grew clearer and brighter, guiding her the rest of the way.

She knew safety was close but her body could not hold out any longer. She swayed, having to force herself to focus or else the path blurred.

Jeb shouted after her, his pounding footsteps getting louder. He was going to catch her!

Virtue scrambled along the edges of the dunes. Not now, she thought, not when she was so close. The house loomed.

'August!' she cried just as Jeb lunged for her.

His arms snapped tight around her waist. When they hit the ground, the dune beneath them shuddered. Parts of it broke away and they tipped to the side, crying out.

His hold upon her slackened as he scrambled for a handhold.

Virtue was closest to the remaining ground. She threw herself forward, barely stopping herself from plummeting to the sands and rocks below.

Jeb went over the edge.

She sat there, stunned. The cold trembled through her but she did not fully register the sensation. Was he truly gone?

A hand appeared and she started. Jeb shakily heaved himself up, clinging to an old, long-dead tree root that had revealed itself in the collapsed dune.

'Help me!' he demanded. 'Virtue, please!'

He looked exactly like the little boy she had once loved as a girl, when he was tripped up by one of his tricks.

Virtue pushed herself to her feet. She stared at him as if she could not quite comprehend.

He was begging now, reminding her of all the times he had saved her from the high tide.

'We're not children any more, are we?' she said softly in response.

She watched as his nails dug into the ground and claw marks scraped across as he was dragged back slowly by his own weight and gravity.

Jeb had forced her into this position. Were it not for her own courage she might be the one lying broken on the ground.

Now Fate had turned it back on him.

Virtue edged closer and Jeb's eyes shone bright with hope. Instead of reaching for him, however, she kicked a stone and watched it plummet to the beach below.

'Are you still a gambling man, Jeb?'

She left, Jeb calling after her, his voice high and wavering. She returned with the long vine of some plant and threw it down.

'Now you'll have a final roll of the dice and we'll see if your luck holds.' The words were jittery from her chattering teeth.

'Virtue, no!'

'It's more than you ever offered me.'

There was a ringing in her head and lightness to her body as if she was slowly relinquishing her grip upon it.

'I have to go home now,' she told him.

Virtue half-staggered, half-ran to the hopeful orb of light coming from Winterton Manor.

Had she but known, she looked like some wispy shred of a wraith returning to its final resting place.

Virtue's Return

August paced the corridors, not caring who saw. His earlier harsh words with Virtue troubled him.

He knew what she was like. Hiding things from her would only infuriate her.

His sharpness had been down to frustration. During the night, while the guests were leaving or bedding down, one of the dogs had barked in a frenzy.

August had run for Imogen's room, pistol in hand. A figure in the dark stood by her half-open door.

August had taken aim and fired. He had not wielded a gun since his Army days. The shot shattered a family heirloom while the man escaped in the crowd swarming to see what the fuss was about.

It had to be one of Strawhouse's lackeys. August was assailed from all corners now.

Imogen thought it a burglar yet she would soon ask uncomfortable questions.

So what if Jeb was her father by blood? August would not let that degenerate get his hands on the girl.

Imogen was August's family. He had cared and loved her for all these years.

Virtue adored the girl as well. Perhaps he was doing both of them a disservice by keeping this from her.

If she knew how her dear Jeb was involved in this, Virtue might be swayed more easily to August's reasoning.

He had gone to Virtue's room planning on telling all but there had been no answer.

She could have gone to bed early . . . if she was an honest woman. August knew otherwise.

The heavy double doors in the entrance hall rattled at the sudden force of someone pounding upon them.

August's head jerked up. He had at least expected Virtue to be discreet and use the servants' entrance.

When his steward emerged to answer August held up his hand.

'I'll greet our visitor.'

216

His eyes were narrowed, lips pressed together. Now he had come to a decision he needed Virtue to understand just how seriously he took her betrayal, even if he would ultimately forgive her.

He unbolted the doors and heaved them open. He glared down at the wan figure on his doorstep.

'Miss Browne —'

Seaweed tangled her hair and bloodied scratches bled down her leg.

She held together the tattered remnants of her chemise, a strap sliding down her shoulder and the hem suckered to her thighs.

She was swaying. Tears and saltwater dripped from the tip of her nose, the skin so pale it was almost translucent and her veins stark blues and purples.

With a cry of horror August scooped her into his arms and hurried inside.

He called for maids to draw up a hot bath, get fresh clothes, bring any fluid that was hot and easy to get down.

His servants fled from him as midges might from the stampede of a bull.

August booted his bedroom door open. Already the servants had pulled out the bathtub.

Someone rushed into the room, waddling under the weight of a pot full of steaming water, and a small waterfall splashed as it was emptied.

There was no time wasted on frivolities such as soap and scent; all that mattered was getting the tub filled.

He focused on the next task at hand rather than on how clammy Virtue's flesh was or how she barely twitched at him combing out the seaweed with his fingers.

He would have preferred it if she had sworn and hit him.

August heaved her into the full bathtub.

Water sloshed over the sides as she sank down.

Before her head went under August quickly kneeled behind so he could keep her above the surface.

He removed her gloves and chafed her hand, feeling resistance upon one of her fingers.

She wore an amber ring — the one he had given her.

All this time, while he had doubted her, might she have been loyal from the start?

He placed a kiss upon her limp palm as an apology.

There was blood blossoming in the water from her scratches. August's throat went tight.

Once Virtue was safe and taken from death's claws he would not rest until he had hunted the smugglers down.

Never mind the law, he should have done this from the start.

Time crept by. Colour entered Virtue's cheeks. Her ragged breaths gentled. Movement flickered just beneath her lashes.

And August waited to see a pair of beautiful grey eyes so full of life open once more.

How Dare You?

When Virtue woke she was suspended in water. She twisted, terrified she was back in the sea.

Warmth engulfed her and a pair of lips brushed her cheek.

'Be still. You are safe. You are home.'

Someone was keeping her afloat in a tub. The person's shirtsleeves were rolled up, revealing slim but muscular arms and a pair of leather gloves. Red and white scars crept just beyond the gloves' wrists.

She glanced up and saw August kneeling behind her, looking down. His hair plastered his forehead.

The green of his eyes had turned dark, the lights in them extinguished by sleeplessness and despair.

'August!' She sobbed in relief.

She turned her head and buried her face into his neck. He stroked her trembling shoulders and hummed soothingly in her ear, waiting for her to calm.

The bathwater had begun to cool but he was so warm and if she held on to him then she might not crumble.

'It was Harold Charles,' she whispered. 'He asked me to follow him, only it was a trap. Jeb appeared and they bundled me in a net. They took me to a ship —'

'The *Reckless Mermaid*,' August interrupted.

Virtue nodded. Her wet hair dragged over his face but he made no move to push it away, letting her continue with her story.

'Jeb is — he's Imogen's father! He threatened me. He has been after her all this time, to spirit her away and start a new life in France.

'His plan was for me to return here, followed by his men, and take her away before you discovered. I would never!'

'I know you wouldn't,' he reassured her. 'I thought he might attempt such a thing. I haven't dared let Imogen stray far.'

'I did not know what to do. The ship's window was open, we were anchored close to shore and so I took the risk.'

He stiffened.

'You could have drowned. You nearly froze to death!' He had been so close to losing her.

Leaning over, he picked up a towel.

'May I?'

It took only a moment for her to consider. Virtue nodded.

As he patted dry her shoulders, she continued.

'Jeb chased me across the dunes, all the way to the manor.'

'Is he still out there?'

She glanced down.

'The ground came away and he fell over the edge. I do not know what has happened to him.'

Virtue relived the scene of him begging her to help within her head. She did not have the words to describe this to August. Nor did she want to.

'So long as you are safe it does not matter.'

Virtue held out her arms and he picked her up, water dripping from her feet and

222

splattering on the wooden flooring.

His dressing-gown was upon the bed. She leaned against him and allowed him to pull the thin layers of silk over her.

The sleeves fell past her hands and the hem pooled at her feet, the woody scent of him engulfing her.

She should push him away. Protest. She was stronger than this.

All her life she had cared for herself, for no-one was ever there to take care of her.

Instead she let August continue, tucking her into the bed.

Trusting another with her wellbeing felt comforting. It seemed nothing could harm her, neither the winds whittling at the windows nor the sea crashing outside.

The ship waiting out there was another world entirely.

As she fell back against the small mound of pillows August drew up a chair.

'Is Imogen safe?' she asked, her voice no more than a whisper. 'I do not know if Jeb's friends will come to avenge him.'

August clasped her hand. It was not as comforting as she wished, as all she felt was the rigid material of the leather glove.

She must have voiced her displeasure for he shucked the glove without complaint.

He was too relieved he could weave their fingers together and feel her pulse beating strongly in her wrist.

'I will send a man to the Yarmouth Custom House. Soldiers will be here by tomorrow to root out the smugglers.'

'Thank goodness.' Virtue shut her eyes.

'Once you have given evidence, a hard-working governess, even if she has been led astray, will be the witness needed to hang them all.'

Her face twisted in incomprehension.

'What do you mean by led astray?'

August's eyes narrowed, a thin vein of anger returning now she was safe.

'Do not tell me you are still loyal to those scoundrels? You might have perished!

'If you will not be sensible then I will have to lock you in this room and force you to give evidence at the trial.'

She attempted to rise but his hands were upon her, pressing her down into the softness of the down-stuffed bed.

She dearly wanted to relent yet could not let this matter go ignored.

'It is you who seems to be acting the fool. I only went with Mr Charles because I hoped to find out the truth!' Her voice was high with disdain. 'You accuse me of all sorts and expect me to button up my lips, sit back and take it all.

'Well, I will not. I was chased across the dunes, threatened, forced to trap a poor animal and was almost drowned, all because you enjoy being so mysterious!'

She was ranting now. Her hands clenched, no longer trembling from the cold.

Instead, indignation stoked itself in the pit of her belly. It kept her warm and conscious and her eyes shining bright.

'I have every right to be furious.

Because I have dared to trust in you have you decided to abuse me so?'

She spluttered out a laugh.

'There has been no subterfuge on my part. I came expecting work, if not a warm, welcoming home and an old friend, yet I thought I had found some like-minded souls.

'Did you believe you stole me away from Jeb to vex him and all this time you have been humouring me until I was conquered?'

August's mouth opened, perhaps to rebuke her or remind her she was quickly wasting what little energy she had regained.

Each time he tried she leaped upon another track so that he could barely keep up with what was tumbling from her lips.

He did the only thing he knew might silence her. He kissed her, swallowing her words.

She was still but made no move to push him off. Instead she relented, parting her mouth for him.

Her eyes were half-shut when he pulled away.

Pleased, he was about to speak when Virtue's eyes opened again, the grey of them sharp as shattered flint.

'No matter my enjoyment of that kiss, Lord Winterton, you will explain yourself to me.

'But first I need you to do something. Do not argue. If that kiss was proof of your affections you'll do as I say.'

Speaking the Truth

August returned, drenched from the drizzle that swept across the dunes. Mud and sand stained his boots, which he scraped on a gargoyle before entering the manor.

He ignored the mess he left behind. Virtue would not be pleased until she saw he had done as she commanded.

With a grunt he shifted the heavy burden in his arms and received a cautious lick upon the back of his hand.

When he toed open the bedroom door Virtue sat up in his bed.

Even though August was soaked, tired and laden with a mass of wet dog, it was worth it as the wan colour of her face lost some of its unsettling fragility when she smiled widely in relief.

'Shuck! I'm surprised he came so easily to you.'

'I have a special touch with wayward animals, it seems.'

Shuck had still been entangled in the

bramble bush when August found him. With Jeb gone, there would be no-one to claim the dog.

At his approach the dog began to wag his tail weakly, perhaps hoping it was his master returning. When he sensed it was another his snout twitched, caught between snarling and whining.

August pulled off his glove and held the scarred flesh before him. At least an animal's eye could not understand the difference between beauty and decay.

He held still, ever patient.

The fearsome teeth were hidden away as Shuck let out a pitiful groaning noise and wiggled while August carefully removed the claw-like twigs keeping the dog prisoner.

Now, he placed the dog in the bath-tub and gave him a quick scrub down to clear the scratches of debris.

He muttered soothing nonsense as Shuck looked at him balefully. There was something comforting about cleaning the day's dirt from the animal, as if sluicing it away meant its earlier trials could be erased as well.

All the while, Virtue watched him. The impression of her eyes was soft and feathery on the nape of his damp neck.

'From your earlier vehemence,' he said, 'I take it you are not involved with the smugglers?'

He made no move to turn. It was better this way as it lessened both of their urges to argue.

'As I've told you again and again,' Virtue replied, sighing, 'Jeb was my friend but he has changed so much I barely recognised him.

'My father has left the inn now, but before that he had got himself involved in adulterating the brandy. I . . .'

She hesitated.

'What is it?'

'Your raid on the inn failed because of me. I heard what your friend, Sergeant Matthews, planned.

'I was so afraid my father would be caught up in the raid that I went to warn him. But Jeb heard as well.'

August forgave her for simply wanting

to protect her father. He understood loyalty towards family.

'What a pair of fools we are.'

He chuckled roughly, scratching Shuck behind the ear and watching the dog's eyes narrow in bliss.

'All throughout our knowing one another you have thought me some rampant pagan while I believed you to be a spy.'

'Yet here I am, in your bed.'

August started in disbelief and turned to look at her.

Her face was flushed. She would not meet his eye, instead clasping her hands together.

'I did not mean it in that way! Only, somehow . . .'

'Even when it is clouded the truth still shines through. Perhaps this is inevitable.'

Shuck took the chance to shake himself and August spluttered in shock, throwing his arms up at the sudden onslaught.

Virtue laughed at the look on the drenched lord's face.

'Good,' he said, even if it meant his humiliation. 'I prefer it when you're happy.'

Immediately Shuck was by Virtue's side, nosing at her.

She petted his head.

'Do you forgive me?'

From the nuzzling she received it appeared he did. Shuck braced his paws on the bed, attempting to climb in with her.

August leaped up.

'Hold, you brute! She doesn't need you crushing her.'

The dog did not heed him. There was only one thing for it. August laid himself out on the other side of the bed, ensuring there was no room for the dog.

Disgusted, Shuck slumped before the fire.

They lay there, Virtue wrapped a little more tightly in the dressing-gown and under the covers, while August was atop them, his hands resting stiffly on his stomach as he wondered if he had gone too far.

'My apologies,' he murmured, low in his throat.

A tremble went through her.

'I think you might have preferred the mound of damp dog.'

'I'm afraid you both smell the same,' she joked, yet she would not meet his eye.

August wondered how to put her at ease. It might be best to get up, leave her to rest and find another bed to sleep in.

Something told him, if he did this, there would be things left unsaid.

They waited until their breathing had slowed into that state just before sleep. It would be easier to admit all and pretend later it was part of a dream.

'Imogen is not your daughter,' Virtue began.

He nodded.

'She is my niece but I am all she knows.'

'Tell me about your sister. I never even knew of her.'

'I hid her from you and Jeb when we were children. I was ashamed.

'Chastity was my twin; we were alike to the same freckle. Our only difference was in our health. She was very small when she was born and the doctor told us she would never reach womanhood.'

Virtue took his hand. He did not flinch or pull away, accepting her comfort.

'I spoke once of an invalid who must not be disturbed. My parents ignored her and the servants were forbidden from gossiping.

'I was a foolish boy, wanting to play with others my age but instead shut in with a weak creature who mirrored me in all but vitality. She frightened me.'

'She must have been lonely,' Virtue reasoned.

August shut his eyes.

'When you left, I understood. Before I was sent away to school I sat by Chastity's side. I read to her, showed her the seashells we collected.

'She loved to hear of the sea and ships in the distance. Almost as if she needed to see them herself she proved the doctors wrong and survived to adulthood.

'After Waterloo I discovered my sister had grown wild, perhaps desperate to experience everything once denied to her.

'She spent her days and nights upon the beach. That is how she encountered Jeb.'

'I know some of this. She led ships to shore with a lantern,' Virtue supplied.

She could picture the young woman standing on the dunes with her light. Trembling in excitement at the coming of a storm as Jeb returned with his jewels and tales of adventure.

Someone shut in for so long could easily be tricked by such a storybook scene.

'Jeb and Chastity married in secret but it was a ploy to acquire her money. He was a brute.

'She escaped the first chance she got but it was too late — she was with child.

'Father forbade her from entering the house. I couldn't stand by and watch her be reclaimed by Jeb. I hid her away in the tunnels.

'Then the storm came.'

She knew where this was going.

'August —'

But he kept speaking. After all this time someone had to hear the truth.

'The tunnels started to flood. While we were struggling to get out there was a cave-in. We were trapped and the stress of it forced her into labour.

'I tried to help, but it was not enough. I was not enough. They found us upon morning, Imogen in my arms and Chastity past saving.

'I hid the truth of Imogen's parentage for fear Jeb would try to steal her as well.

'He attempted to blackmail the family but he did not want to admit his claim to the child. Until now.'

No, Virtue thought. She knew Jeb did not truly care.

He only thought of harming August further by taking his beloved niece. His jealousy had made him ugly and bitter.

Their fingers interlocked. She did not fuss or stroke the scars there; she did not even think he realised in his exhausted state that his flesh was bare.

The gentle motions calmed August. Virtue's eyes were fluttering, ready to give in to sleep's kisses.

Shuck had started to whuffle out snores.

'There is one more thing,' August murmured.

'What?'

'I will tell you in the morning.'

He rolled over. His arm came around her waist, drawing Virtue close.

She should protest, but his warmth was as alluring as sunlight.

There were no kisses upon the lips, only the brush of one over her forehead.

They slept, finally succumbing to their dreams.

A String of Shells

When Virtue woke it was to warmth and arms curled protectively round her.

The rise and fall of breath stirred her further and she realised who she lay with — her employer, Lord August Winterton, who had nursed her back from death and now held her as tightly as a lover.

But could she truly see him that way?

He had kissed her plenty of times, yet it had been to seduce her and turn her into an informant! She did not know what he truly felt for her.

After all this, she wondered, was she going to end up with a wounded heart?

The window-sill caught her attention. Virtue climbed out of bed.

Draped across the sill were a row of seashells strung together. Most were faded designs, the spirals mere impressions. It seemed whimsical in such a severe room.

August woke. His hair had gone askew

and his coat was rumpled. Stretching, he arose and came over.

'I said I'd tell you everything, didn't I?'

She picked a conch shell up and held it to her ear. As brittle and faded as it was, within the mouth of the shell the whispery moan of the sea could still be heard.

'I remember finding this! I was excited because Father would not let me buy a gift for your birthday. You kept it all this time?'

August smiled as his thumb passed over the fractured ridges.

'I used to hide them underneath a loose floorboard in case my father came across them and crushed them beneath his boot.

'Each night I crept from my bed and held them to the moonlight, desperate for day to come so I could see you again.'

Her face was warming. This sounded like the lead up to something she anticipated but dared not hope for.

'We were children,' she replied weakly.

'I was a lonely boy and you were like

239

the sun. After you left the darkness never seemed to lift. Only then did I realise what might have been had you remained.'

'A lord and a teacher's daughter?'

That would still have been less scandalous than a lord and his governess.

Virtue examined the other shells, recognising them. Only one was unknown.

This was a fragment, with jagged sides and a zebra-like marking.

'I found it the morning you left for China,' he told her. 'It broke when Jeb and

I . . .' his mouth thinned '. . . when I fell. 'It was not all I wanted to give you. There was something buried under it in the sand.'

'What was it?'

His gaze flicked to her finger, where she still wore the amber ring.

'It must have come free from a smuggler's treasure haul. I planned to give it to you and make you a promise.'

'But the promise could never be made,' she whispered.

What might their lives have been like

if they had met that day on the beach?

'It is better this way,' August decided after a pause. 'We were too young. Had you not left with your father we might have drifted apart or my parents chased you off.

'I might not have fully appreciated the woman you have become. And you would have tired of me.'

She made to argue but he shook his head.

'I understand how foolish I have been. I hid myself away, jealously guarding Imogen. I forgot how to live.

'No more. I want to be the young man I used to be. I want my niece to be happy. No longer will I be chained by the past.'

That dog Jeb could have stolen another August dearly loved. And he had loved Virtue, all throughout this.

Even when he wrongly questioned her loyalty he could not entirely break away. He truly was ensnared.

If she had meant him ill he would still have been her willing victim.

Needing to be reassured she was well

he leaned over and kissed her cheek. She was still chilled. She shuddered, pressing close.

'Will your changing depend on whether I submit to your proposal?' she asked.

'No, I will not hold you hostage. No matter your decision I will make myself a better man.

'I only ask you remain by my side, as a friend if not a lover. As my daughter's governess.'

He saw his twin reflections in her wide, hopeful eyes.

'But it would not be a submission. Love is a joint game, played again and again.'

She pulled back and grinned.

'Even with your promises you remain a contradictory man. At first innocent and gentle as a lamb, then whispering such wicked things!'

'I only warn you of what is to come. Marry me, Virtue. I do not offer myself as Lord Winterton, the mournful phantom of the coast, but as August.

'I will not hide myself away or keep you and Imogen trapped here. I will live again.'

In response, Virtue kissed him. His arms came up, cradling her to him in relief.

The *Reckless Mermaid*

Two days later a man's body washed up on the beach. Seaweed tangled his limbs, anchoring him to shards of driftwood dredged from the sea floor.

A fisherman found him. Not much remained save for his torn shirt.

No-one could make a definite guess as to who the man was. Most assumed he was a stranger, some smuggler fallen from a ship and abandoned by his captain.

Virtue knew, though. Jeb had not been seen since. His luck had deserted him.

She had come to fear and detest Jeb Strawhouse. She should feel relieved, and in a way she did. He was no threat now.

However, she mourned the little boy she had known. It did her no good but she could not excise it. Was it a weakness?

Holding on to her anger would only keep the memory of him by her side, making him more important than he was.

He would not haunt her.

The *Reckless Mermaid* was still seen on the waters. A message was penned by August to summon Customs and Excise. They would rout the smugglers out once and for all.

It was difficult to concentrate on anything besides checking the height of the sun.

August stood in his study with a spyglass and Virtue sat at his desk.

Soon enough a weight settled on her knee. Shuck had taken to following her wherever she went.

His tongue lolled, drooling on her skirt, as she petted him. At least the shaggy-haired, loping giant calmed her.

'Do you not think it best Imogen is told?' Virtue asked carefully.

She did not relent even when she saw August's back stiffen.

'With what is happening all of it is bound to come out. It would be better if you had some control over how she hears of it.'

'I know,' he muttered. 'I have agonised over this for years. Does she deserve to have all she knows shattered simply because it is the truth? My niece still shares my blood.

'It would near kill me to have her hate me. After I lost everything at Waterloo, after the cave-in, she was all I had. My only chance at having a family.'

Going to him, Virtue hugged him from behind. Her nose pressed against the point between his shoulder blades.

'She adores you, August,' she assured him. 'There will be upset, I admit. She will not understand at first.

'Then she will remember all the years you have cared for her and that will be worth more than anything.'

He turned and she still held on, so ended up with her face nestled into his chest.

August bent his head.

'Still just as clever and sensible,' he said, smiling faintly.

He kissed her, soft and swift, without

fanfare. It was as though they had always done this.

Just as a governess settled and became emmeshed in the household as if she had always haunted it, this romance had crept up on them.

'I will tell her,' he promised, 'but not today. We must focus on protecting her. When I do, though . . .'

'We'll speak to her together.'

★ ★ ★

The coastguard arrived by nightfall. August and Virtue stood at the window, watching as the revenue cutter, *Dawn's Blade*, approached the smugglers.

There were horsemen upon the beach, awaiting any who tried to flee by rowboat.

She settled her head upon his shoulder. He wanted to be out there alongside his fellow soldiers. Only his hands stopped him, for he had not wielded a blade in years.

'I would not feel safe by myself,' she

told him. 'I am glad you are here with me and Imogen, love.'

They could hear the cannonfire, faint booms like thunder. There were flashes of flames. Shadows danced as men fought.

Boats shored up on the sands but they were soon captured. It all happened much faster than expected.

'Who has won?' Virtue asked nervously as August leaned forward. 'Are the smugglers arrested?'

'I do not — wait, they are pulling down the *Reckless Mermaid*'s flag. A red-coat stands at the wheel. Matthews has succeeded!'

The study door creaked open and Imogen stumbled in. Her hair was haloed around her and she only wore one slipper.

'I heard shots. What is happening? Papa, are we under attack?'

August had hoped she might sleep through this. To give her an answer he must explain about the plan to kidnap her. About Jeb and Chastity.

Things had gone on too long already.

The child must know the truth.

Virtue slipped her hand in his. Whatever came, she would be by his side.

Reclaiming the Manor

Lord and Lady Winterton did not have a honeymoon. There was too much to be done.

The grounds swarmed with workers as the manor house was demolished stone by stone, the very foundations dragged back by a team of horses.

Slowly, Winterton Manor was pulled away from the edges of the sand cliffs. The sea would not claim it yet.

The gardens had been expanded, replacing what the sea had devoured.

One spot was left bare in readiness. Soon a school would be built there, catering for any boy or girl who wished to learn.

Amongst all this a new statue had been erected. This stone woman did not recline in the typical classical pose. She simply sat with her head bowed as she read her book.

Oddly enough, it had been called 'The Tigress'.

Imogen watched proceedings from beneath this statue as her furniture was carried on the backs of strangers.

Miss Browne, her stepmother, had promised all would be restored. She trusted her and so did not worry.

Instead, she wondered what the view from her bedroom would be this time.

The most important thing, a portrait of a laughing woman with dark hair and green eyes, was safe. It had been hung up in the small cottage housing them until the move was complete.

Every night Imogen gazed upon the portrait and said goodnight to her mother.

She knew the truth now. What all of it meant was still uncertain. She never got to see her true father but he seemed a distant thing, as easily swept away as seaweed.

Imogen almost believed it to be another girl's story. When she looked at Lord Winterton she did not think of him as her uncle but her father still.

Perhaps it was better this way. He had

cared for her since she was a baby. Surely that was all that mattered?

Shuck rushed up to her. Imogen grinned, shoving her hand into the bag around her waist and producing a ball.

She threw it and he bounded after it. Soon the pair were racing down to the beach.

He was her protector. There was no need to fear any more.

Honeymoon

Virtue stood in the cottage doorway, shawl wrapped over her nightgown. Brittle frost coated the windowpanes yet the sun was rising, heat dripping along the horizon.

Winter would retreat at the approach of spring just as scars dulled over the passing of time.

Arms wrapped around her from behind. Lips settled on the nape of her neck, tickled by the strands of hair coming away from her untidy bun.

'People will see,' she warned with a smile.

'Then come inside,' August said. 'Let them get on with their work. We're supposed to be on our honeymoon.'

'Then go and prepare something to eat. I'm too hungry to do anything.'

Virtue came back inside to the warmth from a fire in the grate. August went to the cupboards and began making his lady's breakfast.

With the manor shut the servants had been sent off to their own homes. For now, the Wintertons lived as any ordinary family. It was doing August the world of good.

Virtue seated herself and watched the movement of his muscles beneath his nightshirt. His hair was slightly unkempt, turned into disarray by her fingers earlier.

He moved slowly, mindful of his pains, and reached for the teapot. She frowned, noticing he had put on his gloves again.

Of course, she did not expect him to discard them entirely. He found comfort in not being reminded constantly and she did not press him.

Instead, Virtue waited for him to sit opposite her. Set upon the table were fresh rolls, little jars of butter and preserves, a pot of hot chocolate and a pitcher of cream.

She quickly fell upon them.

'You'll get jam on your gloves,' she warned.

His eyes were dark, daring her just as he had done in the tunnels. He held out his hand and she met it with hers.

Her fingers crooked around the buttons at the wrist, pushing them loose. She peeled the glove off, throwing it to the floor.

Her kisses began upon his knuckles, travelling over the lightning-white scars that danced over them and dipping between the fingers. Her caresses were slow and gentle.

'There are times,' August whispered roughly, as she tilted his hand so she might lay a final kiss on the centre of his palm where the sunburst wound lay, 'I imagine the scars are coming away with your lips.'

'They are,' she responded.

His other hand was taken up by her and she mirrored what she had already done.

'One day these will not matter to you, as they do not matter to me. Never feel the need to wear these gloves around me or Imogen. We both love all of you.'

He made a soft sound then, something low and sad.

He smiled widely.

'And I love you. For ever.'

He leaned over. Their mouths grazed one another . . .

Then came a bark as Shuck burst in, ball clamped in his mouth and Imogen racing behind.

'You're still not dressed?' the girl complained. 'You promised we'd go to the church tower!'

'And we will,' August said. 'I always keep a promise no matter how long ago it was made.'

He opened his arms and girl and dog leaped into the embrace, squeezing in with Virtue who laughed at the sudden onslaught.

When Virtue had sat in the coach that day, arguing with her father over fossils, she had not expected to discover a family she would cherish.

A place where she would always feel she belonged.

Life, it seemed, was always out to prove her wrong and she would thoroughly enjoy this twist.

We do hope that you have enjoyed reading this large print book.

Did you know that all of our titles are available for purchase?

We publish a wide range of high quality large print books including:
Romances, Mysteries, Classics
General Fiction
Non Fiction and Westerns

Special interest titles available in large print are:
The Little Oxford Dictionary
Music Book, Song Book
Hymn Book, Service Book

Also available from us courtesy of Oxford University Press:
Young Readers' Dictionary
(large print edition)
Young Readers' Thesaurus
(large print edition)

For further information or a free brochure, please contact us at:
Ulverscroft Large Print Books Ltd.,
The Green, Bradgate Road, Anstey,
Leicester, LE7 7FU, England.
Tel: (00 44) 0116 236 4325
Fax: (00 44) 0116 234 0205

Other titles in the
Linford Romance Library:

THE RELUCTANT BRIDE

Natalie Kleinman

Forced by her impecunious father into matrimony with Ernest, the Earl of Cranleigh, twenty-year-old Charlotte Willoughby is widowed six weeks after the wedding. With her fortune under the protection of Ernest's cousin Sebastian, the Duke of Gresham, she begins to enjoy her independence. Charlotte finds herself drawn to Gresham, but he seems cold and indifferent towards her. And when the charismatic Viscount Roxburgh starts to pay her attention, she realises she may not be able to remain unattached for long . . .